I0712470

Just One Mistake

The Billionaire Barons of Texas — Book Eight

Chris Keniston

Indie House Publishing

Indie House Publishing

MORE BOOKS
By Chris Keniston

The Billionaire Barons of Texas
Just One Date
Just One Spark
Just One Dance
Just One Take
Just One Taste
Just One Shot
Just One Chance
Just One Mistake
Just One Family

Hart Land
Heather
Lily
Violet
Iris
Hyacinth
Rose
Calytrix
Zinnia
Poppy
Picture Perfect

Farraday Country
Adam
Brooks
Connor
Declan
Ethan
Finn
Grace
Hannah

Ian
Jamison
Keeping Eileen
Loving Chloe
Morgan
Neil
Owen
Paxton

Honeymoon Series

Honeymoon for One
Honeymoon for Three
Honeymoon for Four
Honeymoon for Five
Honeymoon for Six
Honeymoon for Seven

Aloha Romance Series:

Aloha Texas
Almost Paradise
Mai Tai Marriage
Dive Into You
Look of Love
Love by Design
Love Walks In
Shell Game
Flirting with Paradise

Surf's Up Flirts:

(Aloha Series Companions)
Shall We Dance
Love on Tap
Head Over Heels
Perfect Match
Just One Kiss
It Had to Be You
Cat's Meow

CHAPTER ONE

Some days the opulence of the Memorial Country Club reminded Rachel Baron that despite her ordinary job, her world was one of privilege and high expectations. The gathering of the county's most elite members of society filled the air with the sound of laughter, clinking glasses and as always, the buzz of intimate conversation.

Under the warm glow of the massive crystal chandeliers, she moved gracefully through the crowds in a determined effort to cross the ballroom. Pausing every few feet to exchange pleasantries and air kisses with the Houston socialites who had known her since childhood, she willed her empty stomach not to grumble. Tables of what she knew would be delicious hors d'oeuvres, were getting closer and closer. If only she didn't have to make nice with so many people. The professional upside of being the granddaughter of a former governor, and cousin of a current well-loved senator, included cutting through red tape and accessing hard to find supplies for any of her restoration projects. The downside meant that no matter how hungry she was, stopping to be nice to everyone who recognized her was her only option.

"Rachel, dear. That dress is simply stunning." An older brunette, whose gray roots were well camouflaged and who had been a staple at her grandparents' fundraisers for the many charities her family supported, smiled widely and stepped in for another of those air kisses that Rachel detested. "I love the way the color brings out the green in your eyes."

"How sweet of you to say. You look quite smashing yourself."

The woman puffed up like a peacock. "I had lunch this week at Emily Whitestone's. You did a marvelous job on her remodel. The way you blended the old and new was seamless. Absolutely wonderful."

Now that made her smile in earnest. The project had been a combination restoration of an outdated kitchen and dining room, including an addition that needed to blend in with the integrity of the 1930s home, as well as embrace a modern lifestyle. "Thank you. It was a fun project." She really had enjoyed this particular project, enough to continue politely chatting about it despite the table of food calling her name.

By the time her grandmother's friend had moved on to someone else, Rachel finally reached the table she'd been eyeing all evening, her gaze dancing between the bacon-wrapped shrimp, the caviar fountain, and a few things that she had no clue what they were, but she was hungry enough to sample all of it.

"Skip dinner again?" Her cousin Mitch, the senator, whom she simply adored, came up beside her.

"What makes you say that?"

He smiled. "You're looking at everything the way a kid would eye a banana split."

"Have you tried any of it?"

"The shrimp is quite good and Gwyneth loves the quinoa balls."

Her gaze shifted to the crusty round balls. "Oh, that's what those are."

"One of these days someone's going to serve pigs in a blanket and find a mad rush from us guys who like meat and potatoes."

An eruption of laughter escaped her throat before she could slap a hand over her mouth. Looking over her shoulder, she leaned in and lowered her voice. "I wouldn't mind a few now myself."

"I know of what I speak." Mitch grinned at her. "Changing the subject, I heard that you finished up the restoration in Memorial you were working on."

Rachel nodded. "I did. It's already under contract.

Should close in about ten days."

"Have you heard about the Hartwig house?"

One of her passions was the architectural history of old Houston. The Hartwig House had been an opulent family home, a showpiece along what had once been referred to as Millionaire's Row. That is, until the last Hartwig died off without heirs and the once beautiful old home fell into disrepair. "What about it? Did someone finally buy it?"

"Not exactly." Mitch looked around. "The city condemned it."

"Oh no." Her shoulders slumped with disappointment. Rachel hated the way society so easily tore down older structures to bring in the new. If it were up to the local authorities, all the masterful constructions of Europe would be replaced with new century modern blocks. "That should be a crime."

"That's what I said." Gwyneth sidled up beside her fiancé and ignoring the social norms of public displays of affection, gave him a quick peck on the lips before turning to face Rachel. "Lilian Prentiss told me about the, and I quote, *ugly boarded up eyesore and magnet for every vagrant west of the Mississippi* finally being removed from her neighborhood. So I checked with Councilman Bates. She got it half right."

"What half?" Rachel resisted the urge to cross her fingers and say a prayer for the poor old house.

"The city finally has ownership of the property and the health department and city engineers all agree it's not safe and has to come down. It is indeed on the list to be condemned and razed."

"Shortsighted—" Before she could finish her unladylike thought, her future cousin-in-law cut her off.

"This is the half I think you'll like. The city has a new program offering the opportunity for restoring abandoned buildings and saving them rather than have the city tear them down."

Rachel frowned, running through all the government programs she'd dealt with, wondering which might come into play.

"Anyone willing to restore the homes within one year can purchase the distressed properties for one dollar."

"Wait," Rachel shook her head, "isn't that for low-income neighborhoods? The ones that are prone to meth houses and gang hangouts?"

Still smiling, Gwyneth nodded. "It is, but there's nothing in the program that specifies the size or location of the distressed home, so Mayor Borden is going to add it to the list of homes in the program, unless, of course, you can reach out to him before the list goes public."

The allure of rescuing such a historic gem resonated with everything in her. All she'd seen in recent years was the jungle-like appearance of the old building hidden far behind the walled front gates. If the inside was as bad as the outside, the undertaking would be gargantuan.

"I recognize that glint." Mitch rolled his eyes skyward. "Heaven help us, but I told Gwyneth you'd find such a project irresistible."

Irresistible. He was certainly right about that, but deep down, she wanted more than to simply do the designs, or oversee the restoration. Rachel wanted full control of the project. To ensure that her designs were not vetoed by the owner and that she had the right to hire or fire anyone involved who didn't live up to her expectations.

"Told you she couldn't resist." Mitch wound his arm around Gwyneth's waist. "Am I right?"

Was he right? Could she pass it up? Could she do this on her own? Or was she completely nuts for even considering it? A hard smile tugged at the corner of her lips. "You'd better believe it." Bringing that old girl back to her days of splendor and glory was going to be the most fun she'd ever had!

The Texas sun hung high in the sky, casting its warm glow over the quiet suburban neighborhood where Dylan Schaefer had sought refuge from the relentless demands of corporate life. The canopy of massive oak trees and sprawling green lawns had drawn him to this area of older homes like a desert oasis offering refreshment to a thirsty man. Not that working sixteen-hour days had given him much opportunity to enjoy the lush lawns or blue skies.

Now, the scent of freshly cut wood lingered in the air as he studied the progress of the oak-paneled walls and built-in bookcases for his neighbor's new office. Working again with his hands transported him back to his childhood and days spent helping his grandfather in the workshop. Not since his grandfather passed had he returned to fixing and making furniture, and not till recently did he have a clue how much he loved and missed woodworking of all forms. Especially now, it was nice to, even in the simplest of ways, feel closer to the old man he loved so much. Delighted with the progress, Dylan returned his focus to the task at hand – building a haven of tranquility and creativity for the woman who had been kind enough to notice his car had not left the driveway for weeks.

The sudden and tragic death of his coworker Jim had been the catalyst for changes—big changes. An associate and close friend, Jim was as fixated on the climb up the financial corporate ladder as Dylan. Overworked, and pushing too hard, Jim had succumbed to a stress-induced heart attack at the age of thirty-nine. The wake-up call had rattled Dylan to his core, prompting him to reevaluate the trajectory of his own life. Unable to focus on anything but the loss of his friend, he'd taken weeks of built up vacation time from the hedge fund and spent it rattling around in his own house senselessly until he'd pulled out his tool kit and began tinkering with the lopsided builder-grade cabinets in his laundry room.

From a simple fix-it effort, the project quickly turned into ripping out the cheap cabinetry and rebuilding the area to his liking with solid wood. His temporary departure from the high-stress world of finance had brought him back to a familiar place – the world of craftsmanship and creation. As Dylan measured, cut, and meticulously assembled each piece of wood, the process became a form of meditation, a way to channel his grief and frustration into something tangible.

That was when, warm muffins in hand, Meredith had wandered up the drive and into his yard where he'd been cutting and sanding the last wooden panel. "I didn't know you did cabinetry."

"I don't. Usually."

She ran her fingers down the side. "New kitchen?"

"Laundry. Time for a change."

"May I see?"

At the time he wasn't really looking for company or conversation, but just because he had been in a perpetually crappy mood didn't mean he had to take it out on Meredith. Inside the new laundry room, her eyes had almost fallen out of their sockets. "Holy cow." She ran her hands over the custom cabinetry as if they were made of solid gold. "This is amazing."

He shrugged.

"What kind of countertops are you going to use?"

"Those." He waved at the butcher block counters in an out-of-the-way corner of the adjacent kitchen.

"Where'd you buy them? I have a friend who does restoration work and she's always looking for new sources."

"Didn't buy them."

Her eyes widened, exposing the big white circles around startled brown eyes. "You made those too?"

He nodded.

"Dang. And here I was worried about you."

"Worried?"

"Your car is never in the driveway. You work more hours than Santa's elves on Christmas week."

That particular analogy was almost enough to make him smile. Almost.

"Then suddenly your car's in the driveway for weeks. Honestly, I was afraid I'd find you dead on the floor."

Immediately his mind turned to Jim and how shocked everyone had been to learn he'd been found dead. He wouldn't wish finding his body on anyone, especially not a concerned neighbor. "Taking some vacation time."

She bobbed her head and stepping into the laundry room, fingered the newly glued and sanded countertops. "Don't suppose there's any chance I can talk you into doing some work for me?"

Work for her? Doing carpentry? The possibility of extending his vacation and working for someone else hadn't occurred to him. To his surprise, the thought wasn't a hard no. As a matter of fact, it seemed to sit well with him. Next thing he knew he was nodding at her and as soon as he was done with his laundry room, his vacation time had turned into an indefinite leave of absence and here he was doing a custom office.

With every day that passed, he better understood that the decision to take a hiatus from the boardrooms and corner offices had been necessary for his sanity. When the office was finished, he'd have to re-examine his choices. At this moment, going back to sitting behind a desk, confined within four walls, held very little appeal. Then again, was he really ready to give up everything he'd worked so hard for?

CHAPTER TWO

The expansive windows of Rachel's sleek office offered a panoramic view of the Houston skyline. Always brightening her mood, the central location was a testament to the Baron family's influence. Behind her meticulously organized desk, studying the documents in front of her, her thoughts were consumed by the task at hand—restoration of the old Hartwig mansion.

With permits and the title now bearing her name, Rachel was giddy with excitement over her latest project. It had taken a goodly amount of wheeling and dealing and drawing from every bit of business savvy she'd learned at the hands of her grandfather and cousins to beat out all the other interested developers. At this stage, she had expected to see the wheels of progress continue to turn smoothly. Except for one major fly in the ointment that had unexpectedly emerged, threatening to derail her ambitious plans. Her trusted general contractor had informed her a while back that their last project together was indeed his last project. He and his wife had decided to embrace retirement. In and of itself, that was not the end of the world. She'd been around enough that she could act as her own GC. The real problem was Mike, her best carpenter and crew chief, the linchpin of many successful projects, had fallen hip deep into a poorly marked unfilled posthole and strained his back. Except the strain that had been slow to heal and growing in challenges was now a full on medical emergency requiring surgery, rest, recuperation, and rehabilitation. None of which were conducive to slaving over woodwork and saw horses, and all of which was going to take more time than Rachel had to wait if she was going to meet all of the city's deadlines.

Frustration knitted her brows together as she scrolled through her contacts, desperately seeking a replacement who could match the caliber of Mike, her preferred right-hand man. The remaining *best in the business* that she considered potentially reliable and trustworthy were already scheduled and booked way past her available time frame.

Rubbing her face with her hands, as if that would somehow miraculously conjure a competent and available master carpenter, she blew out a sigh and shook her head. How the heck was she going to pull this off?

A ding on her phone had her glancing away from the papers in front of her. Meredith, a friend since high school, had texted her. Tapping at the screen, the words *isn't it gorgeous!* appeared above a photo. Springing upright in her desk chair, Rachel spread her fingers over the screen, enlarging the image. The last time she'd been in Meredith's office there were four plain walls and no bookcases. Zooming in, she stared at the woodwork. *Who the heck*?

Still staring at the screen, the phone rang. Meredith.

"I was just about to call you."

"Isn't it the most beautiful cabinetry you've ever seen? I mean, it looks like it belongs in the library of a historic estate for the Vanderbilts or Rockefellers or," Meredith giggled, "the Barons."

That was exactly what she was thinking. Only the name Hartwig jumped to her mind. "Who did this?"

"You won't believe it. My neighbor, Dylan. I knew he'd do a great job because of how good his laundry room looked, but this is so much more than I expected. And so affordable too."

That was always a good word to hear—affordable. "Do you know if he's got some time for a new project?"

"Honestly, I think this is just a side gig for him, so I'm not sure."

Side gig? She looked at the picture again. From what she could see, this did not look like the work of a Sunday afternoon homeowner. "I'm in a bit of a jam. Any chance you can send me his number?"

"Sure. He just left my house a few minutes ago. Hang up and call him now before he takes another job."

"You don't have to tell me twice. I'll let you know how it goes." She'd barely disconnected the call when the line was ringing on the other end. Her mind raced with a mix of anticipation and urgency. She envisioned the mansion's restoration as a grand tapestry, every detail painstakingly woven together to breathe life into the old estate. Dylan, if this guy was as good as Meredith's photo implied, could be the key to unlocking the full potential of her vision.

"Hello?" a male voice crackled through the phone.

"Dylan, this is Rachel Baron. Your neighbor, Meredith, gave me your number. Have you got a minute to talk?"

"I do."

Rachel took a deep breath, acutely aware that the success of her venture might rest on this conversation. "I find myself in a bit of a bind. My contractor is indisposed, and I've heard from Meredith that you're quite skilled in finished carpentry. I have a substantial project that requires immediate attention. Would you be interested in discussing the details?"

As the words hung in the air, Rachel couldn't shake the feeling that this unexpected twist of fate might actually be a good thing. Her cheeks tugged at the corners of her mouth. As she explained the situation, Dylan responded with an occasional, *mm hm, hmm*, and a time or two, she could almost swear she could hear him nodding silently on the other end. By the time the conversation ended, he'd agreed to meet her first thing in the morning at the Hartwig House to look over the project. Next thing she called Meredith back, filled her in on the conversation, and arranged to pop over after dinner to see his work first-hand. With every passing minute, she was more convinced that everything was going to work out after all. What she didn't understand is how the heck was there a master carpenter in town and their paths had never crossed?

Dusk signaled the end of what, for Dylan, had been a very long day. Not that he wasn't used to working sixteen-hour days, or longer, but eight hours a day, every day, bent over a table saw or saw horses was giving his back fits. Too tired to even contemplate pulling out a frying pan and cooking something, he opted for fast-food drive thru. Not the healthiest option under the sun, but a large chargrilled cheeseburger from his favorite burger joint across town, along with a mound of golden fried-to-perfection French fries, would definitely hit the spot. Idling at a red light, it struck him unexpectedly that he was just blocks away from where he was supposed to meet Rachel Baron in the morning.

It would take only a few minutes to drive by the address and get a peek at the project before tomorrow. After all, at his desk job he most definitely would have done his homework before dealing with a new client. It would never occur to him to walk into a business meeting cold turkey. Why would carpentry be any different? Turning the corner, he inched down the road, admiring the massive homes behind iron gates and recognizing immediately when he'd broached the address Rachel had given him.

If the weed-covered sidewalks weren't his first clue, the vine-covered walls were definitely a dead giveaway. The first thing they would have to do was procure a good padlock for the front gate. Wide open, one side barely hanging on its hinges, the ironwork begged for every crook, vagrant, and curiosity seeker to wander in and have a look around. Parked inside the property, and standing in the battered circular drive, he took in the imposing edifice. A historic relic that seemed to echo with the whispers of the past, and currently was better suited for the setting of an apocalyptic horror movie.

Thoughts of the daunting task at hand swirled through his head. Daring to make his way deeper onto the property, he stared up at the three-story building, wondering if it was even safe to enter. Turning the corner, he found himself face-to-face with the challenge that lay ahead—a maze of out-of-control vines hiding deep gouges of missing mortar and loose bricks. Despite all the information that Rachel had given him over the phone, not until now had he realized the magnitude of this project. The scope of work expected from him and the time involved, as well as if he was up to the task, weighed heavily on him with each press of his booted foot onto dry and crunching leaves.

Turning another corner, an unexpected force brought him to an abrupt halt. Only the loud groan of the soft wall alerted him to the collision as hot liquid splashed onto his shirt, papers flew, and the warm surface he'd crashed into fluttered backward, arms flailing. Instinctively, his arms stretched forward, gripping the teetering human form. He had not stumbled against the building, or even a shrub, but a very warm and soft and—good grief—Rachel Baron.

Even in the darkening light of day, he'd seen the woman and her family on the news and in the papers enough to realize the well-dressed lady donning thousand dollar boots was neither a vagrant nor a crook. And everything she carried was now scattered across the ground. Way to lose his first big woodworking job. Maybe he was better off behind a desk.

Her eyes widening in surprise, and reflecting a moment of panic, Rachel stumbled backward, swiping at her face where she too had been splattered with what he now guessed had been a hot beverage. "Sorry, I didn't mean to startle you, but you really should watch where you're going."

Those same eyes momentarily flashed anger before a soft smile graced her features and a weary gaze studied him from head to toe before responding. "Yes, I'm sorry, I was distracted." Steady on her feet, she bobbed her head at him and spotted the scattered papers among a red spiral notebook, and a large paper cup from a nearby coffee shop, on the ground.

Glancing at the mess at their feet, she chuckled softly to herself. "I didn't need the calories in the toasted white chocolate mocha anyway."

Belatedly remembering his manners, he leaned over to retrieve the pages at the same moment she did. Heads colliding, both sprang upright muttering, "sorry" in unison, and once again bending over, immediately butted heads again.

To his surprise, she righted herself, and rubbing her forehead, chuckled again. "Maybe we should try this one at a time." Any normal woman should be yelling at him for clonking her on the head—not once, but twice. Why was this woman laughing?

"Sorry. Allow me." He paused just a moment to make sure they weren't going to both retrieve the papers and knock each other out in the process, before leaning over and gathering the notebook and loose sheets into his hands. Returning upright, he handed them over. "Here you go."

"Thank you." Having pulled a paper napkin from the handbag on her shoulder, she wiped at her chest and squinted up at him. "And you are?"

"Sorry. Dylan Schaefer. I thought I'd come take a look around before our meeting tomorrow."

Her smile brightened and her gaze danced across the backside of the house. "Isn't she a beauty?"

A lot of words came to mind to describe the old house. Beauty had not occurred to him. "It is quite a…project."

"Yes." Her smile broadened.

For a second, he had to ask himself, just how hard did she hit her head?

"There is, of course, a great deal of work, and as I mentioned on the phone, we'll be on a strict deadline for each stage of the project. If I fall behind, I risk having the old girl condemned anyhow and losing everything."

"How much is everything?" He looked up again at the brick surface and hoped she wasn't biting off more than she could chew. Though, if her family name was any indication, she could probably find and refurbish Atlantis.

"So far," her smile bloomed even more brightly, "one dollar."

"Oh yeah. I can see where that would be a great loss."

"I did say *so far*. Once I have electricians and plumbers parading through here for weeks on end, the money will be pouring into it."

He resisted voicing *or down the drain* out loud.

"Since you're already here, do you want to take a look inside?"

"Is it safe?" The last thing he needed was to fall through the floor, or worse, for Rachel to fall and break a bone.

Still smiling at him, she hefted one shoulder in a lazy shrug. "So far."

Did this woman ever frown? Until now, he'd considered himself a somewhat open-minded man; after all, he was seriously considering taking on a project that would keep him away from the career he'd sweated bullets for, not to mention paying a small fortune for his MBA, for a very long time, if not forever. "Sure. Let's live dangerously."

That remark brought her low rumble of laughter to his ears and for the first time since bumping into Rachel, it occurred to him that this beautiful green-eyed woman might be more dangerous than the old house.

CHAPTER THREE

Despite Dylan's somewhat gruff first impression, as soon as Rachel saw his workmanship at Meredith's house, the complex and intricate woodworking to make the new cabinetry look as though it had been created back in an era where craft mattered, Rachel knew that Dylan was an answer to prayer. She'd had time to schedule and line up her subs, but this morning, she and Dylan were going to walk the property in daylight. She was hopeful that he'd be able to help her with some of the load the way Mike had.

Sipping on her fresh morning brew, she stood in the second-floor master, staring at all the intricate woodwork. Salvaging it was key to her restoration plans. The entire house was chock full of masterful molding and trims that she'd hate to lose. The cost of casting and matching the work would not only be high, enough of it would be a major blow to her budget.

"Hello," a decidedly manly voice echoed through the house.

"Hello," she called back, hurrying down the hall and stairs. "Sorry. Was lost in thought."

"I know how that goes. I see you got another cup of high-calorie coffee." His chin pointed at the cup in her right hand.

"Guilty pleasure." She smiled. Dylan was dressed in white painter's pants and a light-gray polo shirt with slight splatters of different paint colors. Muscled biceps stretched the fabric of the sleeves. In the dark last night, she hadn't noticed piercing steel gray eyes and thick dark hair cut just short enough to be business appropriate, but long enough for a woman to run her fingers through. A very inappropriate thought for the workplace, but still she found herself staring longer than socially acceptable before tearing her gaze away.

"I'll give you this," the man sighed, "the place looks a little less ghastly in daylight."

"Only a little?" She smiled hoping to tease a matching grin out of him.

His stonelike expression intact, he shook his head. "Barely a little." His gaze darted from the diagonal cracks leading from the corners of every window and doorway to the ceiling then down to the finger-wide gap between the floors and walls. "I know this is Texas, but…"

"Yeah. My foundation guy is coming at the end of the week. He'll be stabilizing the house per my structural engineer's report—"

"Before it crumbles around us," he interjected, his gaze focused on several cracks wide enough to stick, at worst a finger, at best a pencil through.

"I know that's what the city thinks, but these old homes were built to last despite the neglect. Once several new support beams to replace the ones that have rotted through, and shims in a few other places are installed, we won't have to worry about the stability anymore. Then my landscape guy will be here to work on the drainage."

Dylan bobbed his head. "That's a start."

"Yes. With the house stable, and the water runoff no longer settling under the house, I'll schedule plumbers for a pressure test, then we can start fixing these walls. I'm hoping to be turn-key in twelve weeks on the outside. That should keep us ahead of the city's deadlines."

Again, he nodded.

She refrained from adding, *at least that's the plan*, though she wasn't going to tell him that deep down she was a tad concerned if she missed even one deadline after an unexpected setback, there would be a lot of money and effort down the tubes. "First thing will be to remove the trim and baseboards. I'd like to salvage most of it." She wished the man would say something, rather than just stare or nod. "Do you think you can do that?"

The heavy brows shadowing dark gray eyes buckled. Crossing the room, he squatted and ran his finger across a small section of baseboard, the wall and the floor, before nodding again. "I think so, but inevitably, we're going to lose some."

"Understood. Hopefully, with the few walls I'm going to remove, the unused woodwork should offset any losses. At least that's the plan."

His brows remained knitted together, whether because he didn't agree or didn't know if he could do right by the job, she had no idea. If only he'd smile at least once, that would go a long way to bolstering her confidence in him.

The next couple of hours were spent walking through every single room, including bathrooms and closets, as she explained her ideas. Spray can in hand, she marked walls to be removed, doorways to be widened, or doors to be added, along with marking where she wanted switches and outlets for the electrician.

Carefully, Dylan looked at the preliminary sketches she'd done in her graph paper notebook, comparing each one with the actual rooms, occasionally pulling out his measuring tape when he thought she'd made a miscalculation. Of course, she hadn't.

Like her, he carried a notebook filled with notes and hand-drawn sketches. If he managed to string an entire sentence together, she considered that major input from him. Part of her wondered whether, master-level skills or not, she wasn't asking for trouble hiring on a man who contributed nothing to the process. Then again, she wasn't hiring the man for his debating skills. She could do this on her own as long as he turned out to be as good as she hoped.

With every room they entered, Dylan could feel his interest growing. Doubts about whether or not this was the dumbest thing he'd ever done had plagued him most of the night. He wasn't a professional carpenter. Yes, he had some skill, but to take on a house of this caliber, he clearly had lost his mind when he'd agreed to it. And yet, with every step, every brush of woodwork under his fingertips, the doubts slowly faded.

"And this wall has to go. It's a fine line between remodeling and restoration, but a modern family is going to want at least a slightly open kitchen, removing this wall will do that."

Frowning up at the ceiling, he shifted his gaze to Rachel and the spray can in her hand. "I'm no engineer, but based on the footprint, I'm pretty sure the beams run front to back."

Rachel nodded.

"Which means this is a supporting wall. Are you talking the whole wall or some of the wall?"

Her brows collapsed into a perfect v-shape as she stared at the offending wall.

"Don't get me wrong," he continued. "It's not the end of the world, but did you calculate a new beam in your budget?"

Lips that seemed to be perpetually smiling, drew into a thin line for a brief moment before she nodded and the corners of her mouth tipped north again. "I see what you mean. I'll add it to the budget, and the schedule, and figure out how to pay for it. Piece of cake."

Piece of cake. Of course. In the short time he'd interacted with this woman, it was obvious she was a sunny optimist. No one else would consider a major structural change a *piece of cake*, then again, not everyone had the kind of money the Barons had.

"All right. I've got some of the crew setting up a storage area in the old garage for all the woodwork we're going to salvage. Most of the time the doors will be locked so that every Tom, Dick, and Harry isn't romping around in there, trashing my stash."

"That sounds like the voice of experience."

"Absolutely. I've had carefully salvaged trim work destroyed by careless workers who tossed it around or buried it under debris. Once, some idiot tossed it all in the dumpster because it was, and I quote, *old*."

"All right. This is going to take a little time if we want it out intact. I'll get started on the first floor so I can be out of the way when your demo crew arrives."

She nodded. "Great. I've got a few errands to run. I'll be back in a couple of hours."

That sounded perfect to him, he much preferred working alone. Especially now. Some may have considered enough time passing since Jim's death to get back to the status quo, but he doubted there was such a thing as enough time. Right now, he had no interest in carrying on a casual conversation with anyone. He'd barely gotten started peeling away the baseboard when his phone dinged. Since he was in no mood for idle chit-chat with some spam caller, he ignored it and continued slicing through the paint. Another ding and it struck him that maybe Rachel needed something. Taking a second to look, he sighed at his brother and quickly texted: *I'm working.*

The reply came back quickly. *You're not at your house. Where are you?*

Before he even bothered answering, he knew it would mean Derek showing up and probably needing money. Despite his better judgment, he went ahead and texted the address. After all, at some point he needed to pin his brother down and discuss long-term plans for his mother. Though that in itself was a laugh. The words plans and Derek were as incongruent as water and oil.

Not bad, came the immediate response. *Am nearby. Be there in ten.*

Ten minutes too soon for Dylan's liking, and mood. On his knees, he'd never been so thankful to have bought the more expensive knee pads. Carefully massaging, and even cooing at the over-hundred-year-old woodwork, Dylan had removed the first piece without issue when his brother came walking into the room.

"Wow," he whistled. "This must have been some house in its day."

"On that, we can agree." Dylan didn't bother getting up

off the floor, he had work to do.

"You buy the place?"

Putting his tools on the ground, he pushed to his feet, and brushed the dust from his hands. "Nope. Just doing some carpentry work."

Derek's one brow shot up high on his forehead. "Seems like an odd use for that MBA of yours."

"Business is business." He wasn't in the mood to justify his decisions to his brother. He loved Derek, as kids they'd been inseparable like peanut butter and jelly despite Derek being almost five years younger, but as adults they simply didn't see eye to eye on life, liberty, or the pursuit of happiness. "Have you been by to see Mom?"

The way Derek shifted his weight back and forth spoke louder than words. "Not this week."

Where Dylan kept tabs on their mother, the more her short-term memory slipped, the less of an effort Derek made. "Why don't you take her to lunch or dinner? She'd love the one-on-one time as well as chatting up the waitstaff and other nearby customers." His mom had been an extrovert extraordinaire her whole life and a little matter of early onset dementia wasn't going to change that.

His brother's hand swiped at the back of his neck before hanging on, his elbow dangling loosely in front of him. "Well, about that. I'm a little short on cash this week. You know, end of month and all. If you could spot me a few bills, I could take Mom to lunch and have enough left to tide me over until payday."

"Right." Retrieving his wallet from his back pocket, he reached inside and pulled out a handful of twenty-dollar bills, then handed them over to Derek. "Next time I see her, Mom had better tell me all about her lunch with you."

"You know, I love her too." A look of sheer indignation took over his brother's face.

Derek may not be the most responsible adult he'd ever met, but the guy did indeed love their mother as much as he did. "Sorry about that. It's just been a long day and it's not even noon."

"Your problem is you don't know how to have fun."

"Right." He closed his billfold and slipped it back into his pocket. "Has it ever occurred to you that the reason you're always borrowing money from me is that maybe you have a little too much fun enjoying life?"

"Hey," Rachel's voice called from the back door, "I forgot my sketch pad." The second she rounded the corner from the other room and her gaze landed on him and his brother, she came to an abrupt stop. "Derek?"

"Hey." His brother flashed a very expensive smile. A mouth full of caps that Dylan helped pay for.

"How did you find me?" Shaking her head, she lifted her hand at him, palm out. "Never mind. It doesn't matter. How many times do I have to tell you it's over?"

CHAPTER FOUR

Dylan looked from Derek to her and back, a deep frown forming between his brows, but Rachel was too annoyed at Derek to worry about what Dylan thought of the situation.

"Nice to see you too." Derek's flashy smile didn't falter.

The man always was so full of himself. How it took her so long to notice, she didn't understand. Even now, here he was at her place of work with no consideration for her and how inconvenient or unwelcome the visit was. Hands on her hip, she had to force herself not to tap her foot. "Sorry I can't say the same."

Dylan continued staring hard at Derek before closing his eyes and sighing. "I gather you two know each other?"

"Unfortunately," she responded at the same time Derek gleefully responded, "Absolutely."

Again, Dylan sighed and she got the distinct impression something was off. "What am I missing here?"

"I'm not here to see you." Derek took a step in her direction and she briskly took a step in retreat. His thumb flung over his shoulder at Dylan. "I came to see him."

"You two know each other?" The minute the words were out of her mouth she recognized how stupid they were. After all, why would a person come to see someone they didn't know?

"You could say that." Derek moved to where Dylan stood and slapped him on the shoulder in that manly not really a hug sort of way.

Intent on not eavesdropping on her ex and her new carpenter, and lost in thought, wondering how they would even know each other, she didn't notice how close Derek came to her on his way out. "There's still time to change your mind," he whispered, leaning in.

"Not on your life." She took two steps to the left. "And I'd appreciate it if you handled your personal business anywhere but my place of work."

Derek shrugged and making a *tsking* sound, strolled out the back door.

Not till she'd heard the engine roar and disappear as he drove away from the house did she realize she should have recognized his car. So focused on her sketches and swatches, she didn't even realize the absurd muscle car was parked in front. Shaking off the surprise of finding Derek here of all places, she settled her gaze on Dylan. "Not that it's any of my business, but this is my work site."

He nodded.

"How exactly is it that you know Derek?"

Dylan ran his hand across the back of his neck and let his elbow hang, much the way Derek did when he didn't want to answer a question.

A sick feeling was rolling around in the pit of her stomach.

"He's my brother."

Brother. Two peas in a pod. Acorn doesn't fall far from the tree. This was not boding well. She needed an irresponsible, thoughtless, and unpredictable carpenter like she needed a hole in her head. "Wait. Your name is Schaefer?"

He nodded.

"Derek's last name is Alexander. Or did he lie about that too?" Wouldn't that just be the icing on the miserable cake that had been a two year on and off, mostly break up to make up, troubled relationship if she didn't even know his real name. She could add bold-faced liar to the reasons for rejoicing she no longer had anything to do with Derek.

"My dad died when I was two. Mom met Derek's father a year later. A year after that they married. A year after that, Derek was born."

"You're brothers?" Great, now she was babbling like an

idiot. He'd already said that.

"I got the first piece of trim off."

"What?" It took her too long to shift gears and process what he'd said. While she was gathering her thoughts and tamping down the miserable feeling that she'd just made the biggest mistake of her life hiring Derek's brother, he came forward holding a long piece of wood.

"I think with patience we should do well." The guy wasn't smiling, wasn't frowning, was just calmly holding the wood, waiting for her to say something, preferably something intelligent.

She glanced down a minute. He'd neatly sliced the old paint away to help with the removal of the wood from the wall, and it obviously worked. At least he had one trait that Derek did not: patience. The piece was completely intact. "It will have to be stripped and carefully sanded so we can reuse."

"I can do that."

"You can?" She barely lifted her gaze from the piece without moving her head.

He nodded. "I can."

A few hours ago, she would have believed him without a second thought. Now that she knew he came from the same, or almost same, genetic pool as Derek, she wasn't sure if she could believe a word this man said, nor if she wanted to trust him to actually follow through on his promise. What she needed desperately was to get away from here and clear her head. "Let's hold off on that until it's all removed." At least based on the sample in front of her, she knew he could be trusted to do that much. "I really have to run, though."

"I'll be here when you get back."

Already turned to race out the door, she glanced over her shoulder at the man still holding the wood and watching her. Part of her hoped he would be gone and she wouldn't have to deal with any of this, another part of her prayed he would indeed still be here upon her return or she was going to be just plain out of luck.

All he could think regarding his brother was *here we go again.* That man had an uncanny gift for disappointing and ticking people off. Biting down on his back teeth, Dylan resisted the urge to shout out to Rachel's back, *I'm not my brother.* Although he had every intention of cornering his brother after work, to find out exactly what the heck Derek had done to make Rachel so obviously ticked off at him, though he suspected he already knew. Ever since Dylan started making serious money working his ass off at the hedge fund, Derek, who had never been able to finish college thanks to his dyslexia, had tried to compete any way he could. Dating women he couldn't afford had become his modus operandi. If that was the case with Rachel, Dylan had an idea his foot loose and fancy free brother was about to become a good wedge between them.

Before he knew it, he'd removed all the trim in the front room without issue. Only four thousand more square feet of house left to deal with. Looking down at his watch, he realized Rachel had been gone longer than she'd said. Under normal circumstances, he would have thought she'd simply been delayed or distracted or underestimated the time involved in her errands. After seeing the smoke practically coming out of her ears at the sight of his brother, with every hour that passed, he wondered if she was coming back at all, or if he'd still have a job when she returned.

The sound of the familiar ring tone assigned to his mother sounded and he fished his phone from his pocket. "Hello."

"Hi, dear. Your brother said you wanted me to call you."

"You saw Derek?" How about that—his brother did as he said he would.

"Oh, yes. We had a lovely lunch. He took me to my favorite restaurant."

"The Mercury?" He had not given his brother enough money for fine dining.

"Oh." Silence hung in the air for a few awkwardly long moments. "I wasn't in the mood for the Mercury. We went to the Fish House."

As had become the case, he wondered if she truly had not been in the mood for the Mercury, or if she was covering for her forgetfulness. It drove him just a little crazy that he was never quite sure how to take what his mother said. "I'm glad you had a good time."

"I did. Is that why you called? To see how lunch went?"

"Yes, Mom." It took him a moment more than it should have to respond, but he had to bite his tongue not to correct her. What was the point? He listened patiently as his mother chatted on about her meal, the conversation, and what a nice son Derek was taking his mother to lunch. As long as his mother was happy, Dylan didn't care if she had no idea that he'd been the one to suggest and finance the visit. Derek still didn't believe their mother's burgeoning memory issues were, well, an issue. That or his brother simply didn't want to be bothered with the responsibility that would come with their mother losing her memory. Sadly, Dylan suspected the latter was probably more spot on.

What he did know was that he most definitely needed a few words with his *nice* brother. Cleaning up the mess he'd made, he loaded his tools in the car and halfway down the driveway, called his brother.

"Knew you'd be calling. Though I thought it would be sooner."

"Unlike some people, I work a full-time job." At least he hoped he still did. "I'm heading home. Care to take a few minutes and tell me what the hell happened with you and my boss?"

"We broke up."

"Broke up? When?"

"A few months ago."

"And she's still mad. That's a lot of heat for casual dating, don't you think?" Silence held on the other end until he tired of waiting, Dylan prompted his brother. "How long did you date her?"

"Not that long."

"How long is not that long?"

"Two years."

"Two years!"

"Off and on. We may have broken up a time or two in between."

"May have? And this is the first I'm hearing about her?" Two years was an awful lot of time for his brother to thoroughly tick a woman off, but it would explain why until a few months ago his brother hadn't been bothering him so much to subsidize his lifestyle. The Baron pockets were way deeper than his. Crud. "Do you owe her money?"

"Of course not. I may enjoy the finer things in life but I'm not a total cad."

That might be news to Dylan. As tempted as he was to ask for the blow-by-blow description on what had happened, he had the distinct feeling he was better off not knowing. For now, he'd have to keep his head down and work hard in hopes of not getting fired.

Last night he'd come within inches of calling Rachel and telling her that she should find someone with more experience for this project, but as he walked the house with her today, seeing her enthusiasm for bringing the house back to life, the need to be a part of the restoration became firmly rooted in him. He'd had enough sadness in his recent life. The chance to resuscitate something on the brink of destruction filled him with an energy he hadn't expected to feel again. Now all he had to do was figure out how to keep a job that until this morning he didn't even know he badly wanted.

CHAPTER FIVE

"Isn't this a pleasant surprise." Rachel's grandmother leaned over and kissed her on the cheek.

Working over the spreadsheets, blueprints, sub schedules, normally Rachel could put the pieces to the project puzzle together easily enough. Last night, she'd gone over the same thing again and again and still had no idea whether she was coming or going. After a couple of hours, debating whether or not she should risk continuing to work with Derek's brother, she was still just as confused as she had been when she walked into the Hartwig house and saw her ex standing in the middle of a construction zone.

At that point, she did what any red-blooded Baron would do, she drove home to the ranch in the middle of the night and crawled into bed. Though she finally got some sleep, indecision had her awake before the sun shone through the window.

"This may be a first. I don't think you have ever beat your grandfather downstairs for breakfast. Not even on Christmas morning when you still believed in Santa." Lila Baron poured a cup of coffee and took a seat at one end of the table.

Pushing the food around on her plate, Rachel shrugged. "Had a hard time sleeping."

Her grandmother nodded, took a slow sip of coffee, then took a long moment to study Rachel. As a kid her grandmother's scrutiny always made her want to squirm, but as an adult, she found comfort in the way her grandmother always seems to know what she was thinking, and always knew the right thing to say. She just hoped this morning would be another one of those times.

"Something to do with the new project?" Grams reached for the butter dish beside her.

"Something."

"I might need a little bit more information than that."

"You always say the acorn doesn't fall far from the tree."

Grams nodded. "True. But not all acorns become trees."

Served Rachel right for talking in metaphors. What the heck was that supposed to mean? "Care to elaborate?"

Her grandmother chuckled softly. Oh how Rachel loved that sound. As a small child, it always produced such comfort and joy, but right now, it was starting to unravel its magic. "Nothing is set in stone. Genetics predispose us to certain things whether we like it or not. If both your parents have brown eyes, you're never going to have blue eyes. On the other hand, if your dad is a major league ballplayer, there's no guarantee you will be one too. As a matter of fact, there's no guarantee you'll even be able to throw a ball, never mind catch."

Though she had no idea why, that actually made sense. And more surprisingly, it fit her dilemma. Maybe Dylan was as much of an irresponsible jerk as his brother and would let her down, leaving her holding the bag, the same as Derek had done time and time again. She didn't even want to think about all of Derek's no-show dates, and how when he did show up, it was rarely on time. Of course there was also Derek's lack of loyalty. Combine that with a stupidity fueled ego big enough to fill volumes of psychology books—the guy actually had the nerve to ask her sister Leah out on a date, as if there was a chance in hell that her sister was as irresponsible as he was—and hiring Dylan could be a disaster. Or maybe not. If she listened to her grandmother, there was only one way to find out.

Springing from her seat, she drew her arms around her grandmother and gave her a big kiss on the cheek. "I love you. You're the best."

"Glad I could be of help, dear."

Turning on her heel, Rachel ran into her grandfather, entering the room and gave him a big hug. "Thank you so much for marrying Grams."

Clearing his throat, the Governor smiled at her. "Smartest thing I ever did."

A few things were coming together in her mind. Grabbing her purse, she bolted out the front door, down the steps, and hopped into her car. She might even beat Dylan to the worksite. For all of the drive, she rehearsed in her mind what she would say and how he would respond. By the time she got to Hartwig House, she was ready for any scenario to unfold. At least she hoped so.

Pulling into the driveway, she was surprised to discover that Dylan had already arrived. In all of her mental rehearsals, his efficiently already being on the job had not been one of them. After all, Derek had probably been late for his own birth. Maybe this was a good sign that her grandmother was right and even though all acorns came from the same tree, not all acorns bloomed the same. Or maybe she should just forget the stupid acorn analogies and get to the point—was Dylan Schaefer genetically doomed to be like his brother Derek?

Keys in one hand, she hit the fob to lock the car door and braced herself for whatever came ahead. Chin high, shoulders straight, she reached onto the doorknob, turned it, and marched forward. Yesterday the demolition crew had removed all the cabinetry from the kitchen. The plan, before the crew removes the sheet rock in preparation for the electrician and plumber, was for Dylan to take out the wainscoting and baseboards from the adjoining breakfast area. Even knowing that, for some reason it still surprised her to not only find Dylan at work bright and early, but on his knees painstakingly removing and salvaging the old oak woodwork.

Without lifting his head or facing her, carefully tapping away on his tools, Dylan's voice carried across the expansive room. "Good morning."

"Good morning," she automatically responded. Straightening her shoulders, she steeled herself of the conversation she needed to have.

Still tapping away gently at the baseboards, Dylan briefly pointed across the room with this chin. "Didn't know how early you'd be here. Took the liberty of picking up a toasted white chocolate mocha for you. It's on the windowsill."

He bought her coffee? At this hour of the morning, after her nasty confrontation with his brother, the man thought to buy her a coffee? Not any coffee, her favorite coffee. Staring open-mouthed at the man still tapping away, words wouldn't come. This was not in any of her rehearsed scenarios. The only words she could muster came out low and quiet, "Thank you."

When Rachel came in the back door, his nerves went on high alert. Dylan didn't dare look up at her. It had taken all of his self-discipline to casually mention he picked up a coffee for her. For few long and silent seconds, he worried she might actually grow the coffee at home rather than drink it. Especially if she had determined that she wanted no kin of Derek anywhere near her worksite. When the soft-spoken words *thank you* reached his ears, most of the concerns he'd had all night and morning slid away.

Pushing to his feet, he turned to face her. "Figured I owed you one after the other night."

Her head bobbed as she blew into the cup. "I was in a hurry to get here so I skipped my morning coffee." She took a long slow sip. "I needed that."

"So far we haven't damaged any of the removed wood."

"Good." Her gaze drifted from the cup in her hand to the carefully placed pile of salvaged woodwork. "Are you always this meticulous?"

"I try." All his life he knew that attention to the smallest detail was key to the largest profits and success. Whether it was carpentry or the world of high finance didn't make any difference. "I wanted to finish it before your crew arrives this morning. No matter how often you remind them to be careful, demo guys have destruction coded in their genetics."

That brought the smile to her face that he'd hoped to see with the coffee. "I used to think it was a language barrier. Finally figured out there's nothing that can be said in any language to make a bull carefully peruse a china shop."

Both stood silently staring at the walls for longer than would have been likely before yesterday's uncomfortable visit with his brother. Finally, not knowing what else he could do, he turned back to his work. "I'd better get cracking. The crew will be here soon."

"I can help." She set her coffee back on the sill and turned. "I just need to get my tool belt out of the car."

"You carry tools in your car?" That surprised him. He'd had occasion to run into an architect or two in his lifetime and not once had he seen them in anything other than office attire and most certainly not sporting a tool belt.

She smiled at him. "Don't look so shocked."

"Sorry." He squatted quickly and returned to cutting and separating the trim.

A moment later, Rachel came back in, strapped on her tool belt, and stood surveying the area. "How about if I start on the end over there."

Nodding, he forced himself not to mention to be careful, but settled for one suggestion. "Make sure the blade on your knife is sharp. There's a good hundred years of paint slathered all over the place and if you don't cut it clean through, the pressure from the tools will break the wood."

"Understood." She settled across the room and began slicing at the age-old paint.

"You know," he didn't look up, "if it matters, I'm nothing like Derek."

He could sense her freezing at his words.

"I mean, yes, we're brothers. And yes, I love him despite his character flaws, but Mom had complications after his birth and had to have a complete hysterectomy." He paused, waiting to see if Rachel had anything to say. "They say that most of a child's understanding is formed by the time they're five."

"I've heard that." She stopped working and sank back into a sitting position to look at him.

"Obviously, I have no memory of when my biological dad was around, but I know that I had a typical first child upbringing with rules and restrictions and expectations. I don't know if Mom took it easy on Derek because he was a second child or because she knew he was the last child. But as a ten year old, it was clear to me that he had fewer rules than I had at five."

"You remember when you were five?"

He shrugged. "I remember snippets of things, like sitting at the table until I finished my dinner, having to share my new toys with friends at my birthday party."

"And your brother didn't have to do that?"

"If he didn't want to eat what Mom cooked, she'd fix him something else. If he didn't want to share a toy, Mom gave the other kid something else. As he grew, I saw where Mom always made everything easy for him. Too easy." Letting out a sigh, he turned back to the job at hand.

Rachel didn't speak, but lifted onto her haunches and began tapping at the woodwork. After a few minutes, she stopped tapping. "He can be very charming."

"He can." He debated how much to say. "My mother always said he had a tender heart. I didn't understand when he was young, but I get it now. When he puts forth an effort, he's quite the guy, but when he doesn't, well…"

"He isn't." The sound of the hammer banged more loudly than before, followed by a less than ladylike string of words. "It snapped."

Dylan pushed to his feet and walked over. She had indeed snapped the trim work by pulling too hard. "We can probably find someplace for the smaller piece. We'll save it and strip it the same as the others."

Lips pressed tightly closed, she nodded.

"It's okay. Really."

Her gaze lifted to meet his. "Thank you. Mike would have barked at me for a good long rant before deciding it wasn't the end of the world."

"Mike?" For a brief moment he wondered if it was another boyfriend, but unless she believed in workplace romances, it made no sense.

"My previous carpenter. Talented as all get out, helpful as all get out, but a tad explosive at times."

"Is that why he's former?"

She shook her head. "He hurt his back, had surgery recently, and is out of commission for a long while."

"Sorry to hear that, but glad to have this opportunity. It's going to be fun seeing this place come back to life."

"So, you really like the project?" Her gaze softened and he wished he could read the thoughts behind the look.

"Very much."

"You don't like to go shopping, do you?"

"Excuse me?"

She cocked her head to one side. "Do you only wear designer labels? What about restaurant tabs, do you ever pick them up?"

"Of course I do, but I freely admit I have no idea what we're talking about here." No sooner had the words left his lips then he realized what she was asking. Those were all things his brother did. He blew out a sigh. "Derek."

Never in his life had he wanted to throttle his brother as much as he did this very minute. He had a lot of work to do if he was going to convince Rachel that he and Derek were nothing alike. He just hoped he could do it before his brother got him fired.

CHAPTER SIX

Yesterday afternoon, Rachel had spent over an hour tying bright neon orange ribbons around the trees in the front yard that were not to be touched. Before that, she'd argued with the arborist over what could and could not be saved. As far as she was concerned, if there was even a smidge of chance of saving one of these glorious old trees, she had to take it, no matter the cost. Some things were simply worth more than money.

Now, thank heaven, she had the good timing to have arrived just before the arborist's cleanup crew had taken a chainsaw not to the unmarked trees, but one with a hard to miss orange bow. Her good fortune, the word no was relatively universal and everyone froze in place as she screamed at the top of her lungs.

Despite the roar of the chainsaw, Dylan heard her apoplectic frenzy and had come out to stand at her side. "What's wrong?"

Her arm pointing straight ahead at two men standing staring at her at the base of a ribbon-tied tree, she resisted the urge to merely growl. "These men came within inches of cutting down the wrong tree. I have told them more than once the orange ribbons are the saved trees. They keep nodding at me but nobody is moving."

"Doesn't anybody here speak English besides us?"

Her phone in her hand scrolling for the arborist's number, she paused and flicked a thumb in the direction of the man with a machete in hand standing between her and the men working on the runaway vines. "Supposedly him."

"You speak English?" Dylan took a few steps closer to the man.

"Okay," the man answered.

"See?" Rachel again resisted the urge to growl. Where the heck was the arborist's number.

He closed the distance between himself and the crew chief, opened his mouth, and began spewing out words in what Rachel could only assume was Spanish, that sounded awfully fluent to her.

Jaw agape, she almost dropped her phone when the crew chief smiled and nodded, walked to the guy with the chainsaw, rambled for a few seconds waving the confused man away, and hallelujah, the guy with the chainsaw moved to an unmarked tree. She swung around and hands on her hips, looked up at Dylan. "That was very much appreciated. Thank you."

"No problem." He stepped back. "I'd better get back to work inside."

Hurrying to catch up, she kept pace with him. "I know Derek doesn't speak Spanish. Why do you?"

"I told you, I'm not my brother."

"Sorry, yes, but how did you learn to speak Spanish so well?"

He shrugged. "My father's mother is from Cuba. As a little kid, she would always speak to me in Spanish. Then, in high school, like everybody else, I studied Spanish."

"So did I, but I can barely ask for a cup of coffee."

Dylan hefted a single shoulder. "*Café, por favor* will get you a regular cup. Not that fancy stuff you like, but another reason I can speak it now is I did a semester abroad in college. Chose Madrid. I wasn't there a week when something in the back of my mind must have made the connection between my grandmother talking to me until I was five and living in Spain because it was like a floodgate had been opened. I understood everyone and had very little trouble answering. Once you learn, you really don't forget."

"I guess not." She had to hurry her pace to keep up with his long strides.

"I saved all the beadboard in the master bath. I know you won't be using it again, but it's a shame to waste the solid oak. I thought maybe you might have another project some day that can use it."

"Yes. Thank you. I remember the first time I picked up a salvaged two-by-four and found it to be so much heavier than what we buy today at the lumber yard."

"If a house is old enough, then the wood will have been from fully grown mature trees. Today, construction wood comes from much younger trees, so there's less density and it's just not as heavy."

"Yep, that's what was explained to me too."

They reached the back door and he held it open for her—something Derek rarely did. Her checklist in hand, she walked through every room, pleased with the progress they had managed to make in the last few days. Dylan was a hard worker, a pleasant surprise after learning his connection to her shiftless ex. An even nicer surprise was how many other things he could do besides carpentry. He caught the wiring mistake an apprentice electrician had made. Every time someone turned the hallway light outside the master bedroom on or off, the light in the hall closet would do the opposite, and visa versa. Without Dylan taking it upon himself to check a few things, she probably wouldn't have noticed the issue until much further along. A simple correction now would save her a heck of a lot of time and money later.

She'd been sitting in what would be the new master bathroom, measuring and sketching out the details now that she had a better vision of the space in the empty room. As usual, she'd lost track of time when she heard heavy footsteps approaching. The tapping on the nearby doorway had her looking up.

"It's lunch time." Dylan pointed to his watch. "All the crews are set up eating under the trees in the front yard."

Shaking her head, she set the notebook down on her lap. "I didn't bring lunch."

"I noticed you never bring lunch and rarely stop to eat. I made a couple of meatball heroes with leftover from dinner last night. I brought extra for you. You should really eat a little something,"

"You brought me lunch?" She was sure her mouth had

fallen open again. Twice in one day he'd surprised her. Twice in one day she realized how wrong she'd been to paint him with the same brush as Derek. When had she become such a rotten judge of character?

Dylan felt one side of his mouth tip up at the expression on Rachel's face. Anyone would think he had just gifted her with a 2-carat diamond ring on their first date. "Don't look so surprised. It's only a sandwich."

She reached out to accept the proffered foil-wrapped sandwich. "Thank you."

"The front yard seems to be taken, but it's a beautiful day outside. There's lots of shade in the backyard."

Still sporting a slightly stunned look, Rachel nodded. "Outside would be nice."

To make eating outside even nicer, he walked ahead of her, and pulling a rag from his back pocket, wiped down an old metal table with circular benches that tilted sideways under the biggest live oak in the yard. "If you'll have a seat, my cooler is in the truck. I'm afraid I don't have any toasted white chocolate mocha, but I'll grab us a couple of waters."

The corners of her mouth lifted in a quiet chuckle. "Water will be nice, thank you."

Relief washed over him when his impromptu remark about the coffee made her chuckle. The moment the words left his mouth he wanted to kick himself, afraid it would tick her off even more. It was bad enough he couldn't do a darn thing about who he was related to, the last thing he wanted to do was irritate her. He'd have to be more careful because next time might not go over so well. Leaving his sandwich on the table, he trotted over to his truck in the driveway, pulled out his cooler, and rummaged in his glove compartment for a couple of napkins, then hurried back. "Here we go."

Rachel was already unwrapping the sandwich.

"It tastes better when it's warm, but we don't have a

microwave set up in the house."

Her fingers wrapped tightly around the whole-grain bread, she took a bite and for just a second, he almost saw her eyes roll back in her head. "Oh wow, this is seriously delicious." A drop of red sauce dripped on the edge of her mouth, and like a true well-bred aristocrat, rather than use her finger or lick it off, she gently dabbed at the spot with the napkin.

For the first time since speaking with her on the phone that first day, he was acutely reminded that despite his success, she came from a very different world than his middle-class upbringing.

"Tell me," she leaned her wrist on the table, the sandwich half eaten, "where did you buy this? This has to be the best meatball sandwich I have ever had. My grandmother's cook, Hazel, does amazing things. But even her red sauce isn't this good."

He swallowed a mouthful, took a quick sip of water, and shrugged. "I didn't buy it. I made spaghetti and meatballs this weekend. The meatballs are leftovers."

"You cook?" That look of surprise was back on her face.

"Don't you?"

"Well, yes. But not like this." She waved the sandwich in front of her, moving the foil wrapper further down. "What brand of sauce do you use?"

Swallowing another bite, he shrugged again. "My New York born and bred Italian mother would shoot me if I bought sauce in a jar." This time he may have gone too far, she almost choked on the bite she'd taken. Gently patting her on the back, he hoped he wasn't going to have to do the Heimlich maneuver. "You need more water?"

Hand on her chest, she swallowed hard and shook her head. "Let's just say, if I thought you surprised me before, making spaghetti sauce from scratch takes the grand prize."

What was a guy supposed to say to something like that? Most of the time he felt like he was walking on eggshells around her, afraid to say the wrong thing.

"Would it be safe to guess that you enjoy cooking?" she asked.

"I suppose I do. Until recently, my job at a hedge fund consisted of a great deal of stress and a great many hours a day. Once I got home, I could have slipped something in the microwave, but I found early on that cooking relaxes me. Helps with washing away the stress of the day, leaving my job behind for just a short while. Mom had taught me the basics, and in today's world, with video cooking demonstrations on your tablet, your television, or your phone, it was easy to learn more about cooking."

"Wow." She pulled one foot up and tucked it under her other leg. "How come Derek doesn't cook?"

Wasn't that the $64,000 question? "I honestly can't tell you. Mom tried. I'm pretty sure he knows how to use a can opener, the microwave, the coffee pot, and can probably boil water for spaghetti, but if I remember correctly, his meal of choice is those noodle in a bag soups that he mastered in college."

Tinkering with the last of the sandwich and surrounding aluminum foil, she looked up at him through very long lashes. "Confession time."

He braced himself, hoping whatever she had to say wasn't going to have him packing his toolbox.

"My grandmother, in her ever-quaint way, told me—no, reminded me—that rarely are siblings all the same."

"Sounds like a smart woman."

Smiling, she waved her hands in the air. "Actually, she spoke in metaphors about acorns and trees, but the gist was the same. Every day since I learned you and Derek are related, I keep expecting you to do something to remind me that you are Derek's brother."

Watching her shake her head, he knew her next words would either make or break his day. Using every inch of skills developed in the business world to never let them see you sweat, he tried not to even breathe as she spoke.

"Every day, you have proven my grandmother right. Bottom line, I owe you an apology. I am terribly sorry for assuming the worst."

Whether speaking his mind now was a good or bad thing, only time would tell. "For what it's worth, whatever my brother did, on behalf of my entire family, I apologize."

Staring at him, her head tipped to one side just enough for a distracting ray of sun to peek through the branches and shine on her already golden hair.

"If it makes you feel any better, I'll be happy to beat him up for you," he teased.

That got him the reaction he had hoped. Her foot fell out from under her, and she nearly doubled over laughing. "I don't think that will be necessary. Thank you for the sentiment."

Her smile was downright infectious. Whatever his brother had done, only one thought stood out in his mind, Derek was a complete and total fool.

CHAPTER SEVEN

T he last couple of days at the job site could not have gone more smoothly. Dylan hadn't realized how large the elephant in the room had been until it was gone. Every day, Derek had been in the room regardless if he actually showed up or not. Ever since the lunch date in the backyard, the tension had diminished. The perky, smiling, happy woman was back. A smile was regularly on her face. He found himself looking forward to the times she came by the job site, even if she was awful at removing delicate woodwork.

As he pulled into the driveway, he was surprised to see Rachel's Beamer parked in front. Stepping out of his new pickup, he slammed the door behind him at the same time Rachel slammed her door behind her, a huge smile on her face. "Morning."

"Morning." He met her in the middle of the yard.

Holding what he recognized to be the coffee cup from her favorite coffee shop in one hand, she held out another cup. "Cream and one sugar, right?"

She'd brought him coffee? And the way he liked it too. "For me?"

"It's not for Julio." Her grin shifted to a chuckle. "Though if you don't want it, I think I saw him drinking coffee the other morning."

For the first time in a long time, he actually felt like smiling. "That won't be necessary. I'd love a cup. Thank you." Taking a sip of the just hot enough coffee, he found himself thinking that Julio could find his own girl. Wasn't that absurd. After all, Rachel wasn't his girl. "What brings you here so early?"

"I forgot my notebook yesterday and I needed some measurements to complete the plans for the city permit department."

"Is that going to take long?" He pulled out his keys.

Rachel stood behind him as he put the key in the lock. "No. At this point I know most of the folks at City Hall better than my own family. It shouldn't be a problem."

The door flew open and Dylan stopped in his tracks, staring down at the wet floor. "What the…"

"What's wrong?"

"Holy…" Dylan hurried inside, sloshing through a steady film of water. "Something's leaking. I'll check the master bath."

"Wait." Standing in the middle of the foyer, Rachel pointed straight ahead to the staircase. "They're wet."

Not stopping to ask questions, he bolted across the room and took the stairs, two at a time.

Rachel hurried behind him.

"Oh, crap." Water poured from above the central hall ceiling. Soaked sheetrock had collapsed and now covered the hallway and game room floors along with soggy pink insulation. "This is too much for the a/c unit. Has to be the water heater." Without waiting for Rachel's response, he turned and flew down the stairs and across the house. Hurrying to his truck, he pulled out a water key, then proceeded to the front yard and turned off the water.

"I have towels in my car." Rachel ran past him.

He shook his head. "You're going to need more than towels for this mess. I spotted a wet vac in the garage. You go back inside and check that the water isn't running anymore."

"Got it. We have to save the floors."

The floors. Who knew how long that water had been running. Under all that soggy insulation, it might already be too late to salvage them.

The water vacuum in hand and a garden hose over his shoulder, he was at the back door when Rachel came hurrying out. "The water is off to the rest of the house but the tank is still gushing."

"It's not going to stop until the tank is empty. That's a fifty-gallon water heater. I'll attach a hose and divert what's still in the tank outside, then start vacuuming; you go to the store and pick up all the large fans you can get your hands on." He tossed her his keys. "Take my truck. That little Beamer of yours won't hold enough."

She turned on her heel and ran to the driveway.

He hoped she hurried. This was going to be a royal mess, and it didn't take someone of his financial background to do the math. If all the original hardwood floors needed to be replaced, the budget on this place was going to go through the roof.

Lugging everything upstairs, he hung one end of the hose out the back window before pulling down the ladder in the hall and carrying the opposite end of the hose upstairs. In the attic, he could see where the bottom of the tank had rusted through. Struggling to attach the hose to the rusted spout, he finally redirected some of the water and hurried downstairs to make sure the solution worked the way he'd planned. Water slowly draining into the backyard, he'd managed to bag half the soaked insulation when he heard Rachel stomping quickly up the stairs.

"I got the five big fans and two little ones and another vac. I figure if we need more fans I can always go to a different store." She scanned the room and before he could say a word, she was leaning over and scooping up the insulation alongside him.

"Start vacuuming. The insulation will make you itch."

She shook her head. "We need to get this stuff out of here first or it will just drip all over the vacuumed floors."

"I've got this part. You go vacuum."

All she did was shake her head. She was right and he knew it, but he also knew that the itch from fiberglass insulation was a bitch. "Please."

Tying the bag, she straightened and shifted to the side. "This is no time to be stubborn. If two hands are better than one, than four are better than two."

There was no point in wasting their energy arguing. All he could do was keep working as fast as he could. Another few minutes and they had ten garbage bags filled with debris tossed out the side window.

"I'll start vacuuming up downstairs." She didn't wait for him to respond, just turned and ran down the stairs while he flipped on the vacuum he'd carried upstairs and began sucking up the water.

Next thing he knew, the water was almost gone and Rachel was hurrying back up the stairs, a large fan in each hand.

"Let me get that." He reached for one and she actually rolled her eyes at him.

"I carried them this far, another few feet won't kill me. Keep vacuuming. I'll set them up. I also turned up the a/c."

"Pull the humidity. Good idea." Not wanting to waste time arguing, he went back to vacuuming up the water.

The fans set up and the water mostly vacuumed, Rachel was back at his side, down on all fours, wiping the damp floors with towels, trying desperately to get rid of as much water as she could. For a rich socialite, this woman knew how to work hard. And without complaining. He had to admit, even though he knew she wasn't afraid to roll up her sleeves and help, this degree of teamwork had surprised him. The realization made him wonder what other surprises might she have in store for him?

Hands at the base of her lower back, Rachel stretched left then right. Together, she and Dylan had cleaned up, soaked up, and rubbed down every inch of wooden flooring in the house. She could already see where in several places the edges were beginning to curl up. When the house and floors fully dried out, if she and Dylan had moved fast enough, the hardwood planks should flatten again. If not, hopefully they wouldn't curl up any more and this hint of cupping could be sanded even. Whichever, the next few days would tell.

"Not how I expected to start the day." Dylan re-entered the home from placing the vacuums in the garage. "Good thing it's not cold out or the a/c would be almost as unpleasant as mopping up the mess."

"I really appreciate the help. That wasn't in your job description." She ran her hand around the back of her neck, failing miserably at loosening the kink.

"We didn't have any choice. I'm sure if Julio and the others had been here sooner, they would have done the same."

"If I could communicate with him," she chuckled, still hanging onto her neck.

"Some things are international. No need for translations. Gushing water from a broken water heater is one of them." Footsteps fell behind her, moments before strong fingers replaced her hand. "Relax."

That was easier said than done. The warmth of his breath fanning against her neck had her senses on high alert while his thumbs dug into her aching muscles and her skin tingled under the gentle touch of his fingers. She sucked in a long, deep breath and blew it out just as slowly. Her shoulders fell, and the more his fingers worked her stiff shoulders, the more she was indeed able to relax.

"That's better."

"Any better and I'm going to melt into the floor." Reluctantly, she stepped forward before she became so relaxed her legs turned to jelly. "Thank you. That helped."

"I'm afraid your notebook didn't bode well." Dylan had crossed the room and handed her the damp spiral-bound book. "Somehow it wound up on the floor of the master."

"That's odd." She was sure the last place she'd had it had been upstairs working on the new bathroom. It was why she needed it now to complete the second floor plans to submit to the city council as well as the permit department in time to meet her next deadline. The dollar project didn't allow much time for each rehab stage. Probably to keep people from milking the system. "I might have to go home and stick it in the oven."

"Oven?" One eyebrow shot up high on his forehead.

She couldn't stop from laughing at the shock on his face. "Surely you spilled a drink of some sort on a notebook in school and needed to dry it out fast?"

"I suppose, but I have an aversion to setting houses on fire."

"I'm not going to leave it in there long enough to set anything on fire, but it will dry out faster so I can use the numbers."

"You never cease to surprise me." He shrugged and shook his head. "Anyone else and I would have my doubts, but something tells me you're going to have a dry notebook and finished architectural plans in no time at all."

"Thank you. I think." She held the wet book away from her and turned toward the back door. "I'd better get going. Will try and stop in later today if I can. Call me if anything else pops up."

"Will do."

Pulling the back door closed behind her, she watched as Dylan crossed the room to return to work. *You'll have finished plans in no time at all.* His confidence in her made her want to puff up like a peacock. How had she ever even considered this man would be like his brother?

CHAPTER EIGHT

Of all mornings to have to deal with a flat tire. Dylan knew that the city project inspector was coming by some time today and he wanted to make sure that everything was ready for him. They'd been pushing hard to make this week's deadline. He hadn't said anything to Rachel, but he'd been keeping an eye on the plumbers and electricians and anyone else who came through the house. They were coming in under the wire and even though he was technically just the carpenter, he knew enough to make sure everything was done right.

Rachel had been trusting her plumber, and her electrician, and all her other subs, but 'her' electrician was rarely the one who showed up. The work was done by his crews. Several who didn't speak a lick of English and would not be the best people to interface with the inspectors.

Thankfully, he pulled into the driveway and the only other vehicle on site was the truck of the guys redoing the sheetrock. They were almost done with the garage and if the electrical and plumbing didn't pass inspection today, Rachel was going to have a crew of workers sitting around twiddling their thumbs, unable to close up the walls.

Making his way to the garage where he'd been working on the kitchen cabinets, he heard an engine pull up. All he needed was a quick glance to know it was the inspector. Where was Rachel? Halfway across the lawn, he spotted her Beamer flying down the street.

"Morning." She smiled up at them. "Sid, it's nice to see you again."

"Rachel." The inspector extended his hand to shake

hers. "Quite the project you have going here."

"One of my most challenging."

"I heard this one came within inches of being torn down."

She bobbed her head, and Dylan shoved his hands in his pockets. Something about the way the guy kept grinning at her, or more the way he almost leered at her, had Dylan wanting to literally knock some manners into him. For the next hour he shadowed the two, occasionally offering information that Rachel didn't have at her fingertips.

When they walked into the garage in search of the panel box, Sid stared, eyes narrowed, at the brand spanking new box. "These are the wrong screws."

Screws? Dylan squinted over the man's shoulder.

"These are sheetrock screws, they could be dangerous." Sid paused and glancing at Rachel, shot her a soft and too-friendly smile. "I should red tag you for this."

For just a second, Rachel's eyes opened wide before she quickly composed herself, hiding that momentary flash of panic. "I'm sure we can get that taken care of quickly. When can you come back?"

"Not for at least another week."

"But my deadline is this Friday. This is my first time on one of these special deals. How strict is the deadline?"

The inspector raised his brows and tipped his head in an I'm sorry gesture. "Pretty strict."

Now panic truly shimmered in her gaze for anyone to see.

"Excuse me a second." Dylan turned and trotted easily down the drive to his truck. Leaning into his large tool box, he rummaged through one section in search of screws that would meet this guy's standards. He was always fixing something or other at his house and knew he had to have something that would work. Down to his last compartment, score! Exactly the four screws he needed. Grabbing a standard flat head screw driver rather than use his drill, he hurried back.

Sid was still apologizing to Rachel, and if Dylan was reading the room correctly, the guy was prepping to leverage an inspection pass for a dinner date, or something else he didn't want to think about.

"I think I have a fix." Dylan handed the four screws to Rachel and without waiting for a response from either of them, proceeded to loosen the offending screws.

"Perfect." Grinning like a kid on Christmas morning finding the cookies and milk all gone, she held her hand out, palm open, for Sid to see. "One more minute and you can reinspect."

Dylan grabbed the first screw and put it in place.

"See?" Rachel waved at the panel box as Dylan screwed in the second screw.

Poor Sid didn't look very happy, but he did look smart enough to know if he dug his booted heels into the ground and didn't pass the panel box, he'd never get a date with Rachel. "Just let me sign off on this and you'll be all set until the next step."

Rachel smiled at Dylan and when Sid wasn't looking, winked at him.

As Sid stood by the city truck a few minutes later, waving at Rachel, they waited for his truck to pull away from the curb and make its way down the street.

The moment the truck turned the corner and was out of sight, Rachel spun around and threw her arms around him. "Thank you, thank you, thank you. You literally saved the day and this project."

So caught by surprise at her enthusiasm, all he could do was grunt. Just as quickly as she flung herself at him, she pulled away doing a little jig in place and Dylan found himself wishing she'd come at him again so instead of standing statue still, he could at least return the hug. Not for the first or last time, he couldn't help but think what an idiot his brother was for letting this woman get away.

Rachel was so darn happy, she could just kiss Dylan for saving the day. "That was so close."

Silent, Dylan simply nodded.

"Seriously. I owe you."

"Just doing my job."

Her grin widened. "That was more than your job. Thank you."

"You're welcome."

For some reason, she knew she should get going, but her feet weren't moving.

"When is the flooring guy scheduled?" Dylan glanced over her shoulder at the garage, then back.

It took her a few seconds for her mind to shift gears. "Now that we have the inspection signed off on, the guys can start closing up the walls and texturing. Then I have the painters coming, then the floor guys."

Dylan started walking toward the house. "Do you want the cabinets installed before the floors are in or after?"

"I prefer after. I think it's kinder to the homeowners if they make any changes they have flooring underneath. Besides, I hate quarter round under cabinets."

"Agreed." He nodded. "Do you want me to paint the cabinets while the others are working?"

She stopped at the back door. "You paint?"

"Did you not want me to paint the cabinets?"

Considering how stellar Meredith's library turned out, had she wanted the kitchen stained she most definitely would have asked him, but it had not occurred to her that he might be able to paint them. "Are you as good at painting as you are at staining?"

The man actually chuckled. "If I said yes, would you believe me?"

Would she? If it were Derek, most definitely not. She might have the first year they dated when he had her fooled, but eventually even she figured out the man spoke with a forked tongue. "Yes, I believe I would."

"Does that mean I'm painting?"

"I think it does." She had a great painter, and reasonably priced too. But she liked the idea of having Dylan on the site more than less.

"Then as soon as I'm done with what I'm working on

now, I'll start spraying the cabinets. That way we can install as soon as the floors are in. This way we won't have to tape everything off and touch up walls." He paused by the fridge near the back door that they kept plugged in to keep food and drinks cold for the crews. "I didn't bring any coffee this morning. Want some carbonated caffeine?"

"Actually, a cola would be nice."

He opened the door, reached for a six-pack of colas and handing her one, frowned.

"What's wrong?"

"I put a full package of muffins in there yesterday afternoon. Ate one, maybe two, but there's only one left."

"One of the other workers?" she asked.

"Maybe."

"You don't look convinced."

"From what I've seen around here, these guys don't usually take what's not theirs without asking, and they favor stuff their wives or mother made." Shaking his head, he shrugged. "You're probably right. One of them must have been a fan of blueberry muffins. Would you like one?"

She shook her head. "Thanks, but you can have it." Offering her the last muffin said a lot about a man. This was something she could see her brothers doing. Though it still made no sense to her how his mother had raised him right and missed the mark with Derek.

"Do you hear something?" Dylan stopped dead in his tracks.

"No?" She stood equally still. "What kind of something?"

He shook his head and held up a finger. A small squeak sounded and he practically shouted, "There."

Listening as hard as she could to the silence in the room, the faint noise sounded again. "What is it?"

Moving slowly in the direction of the squeak, Rachel practically tiptoed behind him as they crossed the room, following the sound. If the man stopped short, she would without a doubt plow very ungracefully into him.

The back door had not latched fully shut so it took a moment to realize the noise was actually coming from outside. Once standing in the backyard, the sound was louder and more frequent. Like a pedigree dog on point, nose to the air, Dylan followed the sound to the side of the garage. "Well, look at you."

Two small kittens, huddled together, meowed, and Rachel would swear they were looking directly at Dylan every time they opened their mouth. "I wonder where mama is?"

"I was just wondering the same thing." Dylan squatted down on his haunches and leaned forward, using his one finger to rub the top of their heads. "Usually feral kittens run. They must be too young to have developed the protective flight instinct."

"Do you think their mother is around?"

He shook his head. "We've been working here for over a week and today is the first time we've heard them. Either mama just moved them here, or she's gone."

"Oh." Rachel's heart actually hurt. She wasn't stupid, she knew there were shelters filled with abandoned animals, but she'd never run across such defenseless little ones before.

"I'll be right back. Make sure they don't run away."

From what Rachel could see, these kittens had no intention of moving, but she'd gladly watch over them. Another few minutes and Dylan reappeared with a plastic bowl. "Is that milk?"

He nodded. "Julio keeps it in the fridge for his coffee."

The second he set it down, the two fur balls hurried over and began lapping as if they hadn't been fed in ages.

"At least they're old enough to drink from a bowl."

"What do we do now?"

"Get a little food in their bellies and then watch and see if mama comes back."

She knew that made sense, but she wasn't over joyed with leaving the kittens out in the elements.

Once again rubbing his finger along the top of their heads, Dylan almost cooed at the pair. "Eat up, fellas, your mama should be back."

Mentally she was shaking her head. When did this grumpy man who so sparingly smiled develop a soft side?

CHAPTER NINE

"They're gone!" Just about mid morning, Rachel came bursting through the back door, smiling like a loon. "The kittens aren't there any more. Do you think mama moved them?"

"Not hardly." With a lift of his chin, he pointed to a cardboard box across the kitchen and waited for Rachel to walk over.

Her smile grew even wider. "You brought them inside?"

"Last night I was worried that it was getting too cold for them so I came by to check on them. They were still curled in the same spot. No sign of mama, so I put them in the box in the same spot by the garage with a little newspaper under a towel for insulation. This morning there was still no sign of mama but the two made it pretty clear they were hungry, so I brought them inside."

"I wonder what happened to her?"

"Could be anything. A coyote could have gotten her. Some kind neighbor may have taken her in not realizing she had kittens somewhere, or one of those feral cat organizations could have caught her and taken her in to be neutered, or taken her to a shelter if she's as friendly as her kittens."

He kept his gaze on Rachel as she dropped to a sitting position beside the small box and reached inside to stroke the kittens. From his years working with very prominent and wealthy people, he'd never met anyone with as much money and reputation as the Barons who showed as much down to earth kindness as Rachel. Most of the time it was hard to remember she was a Baron. The family name was the closest thing this state had to royalty. Their names appeared in the paper all the time affiliated with some charity or project to benefit mankind in general.

"What's this?" Still smiling, Rachel turned to face him.

"What's what?" Why he pretended he didn't know what she was talking about was dumb. Obviously, he was responsible for the kittens' current condition.

"Uh, they're resting on a fleece pad." The bridge of her nose crinkled as she reached deeper into the makeshift feline home. "And it's heated."

He shrugged. "I thought they'd feel more like they were with their mother if the cat bed were warm."

The frown had shifted to a tight-lipped smile. "You don't think the fleece alone would have done that?"

No point in answering, he'd already been busted, a lazy shrug would have to do as a polite response. He might as well fess up to all of it. "I bought them collars too."

"Really?" She returned her gaze to the box.

"Haven't put it on them yet. Thought I'd give them a little time to adapt to the box before I manhandled them again."

"I see." She reached in and lifted one kitten out of the box. Immediately, as it snuggled into the crook of her arm, the other one protested loudly to the absence of its sibling. "Oh, dear. Do you want out too?"

The next thing he knew, the two kittens were bouncing around doing what he thought of as kitten wrestling, before chasing after a small wad of paper they'd found on the floor. His first thought was that a construction site was not the safest place for kittens to be playing, but the bright grin on Rachel's face as she watched the two dart about frolicking was enough for him to keep his mouth shut, and maybe put down the paint brush.

"Oh no." Rachel sprang to her feet and trotted over to where one kitten had strolled onto the face up paint can lid. "This is not a good idea for little kitties." Grabbing the cat around its middle, Rachel did her best to hold it out so as not to get paint on anything else. Too bad the kitten had a different idea. Quickly squirming out of her hands, the little thing crawled up her front and over her shoulder, studying how to get down.

Hurrying across the room, he pulled the kitty off of her and cradled it tightly against him, then leaned down and picked up the lid before the other kitty discovered it. Spinning around, he looked at her turquoise top covered in tiny white paw prints. "Your shirt is ruined."

Tugging on the hem, she pulled the shirt away from her, and dipping her chin, stared down at it. "Nah. It's just an artistic fashion statement. Paw prints can be all the rage."

"Doesn't anything ever upset you?" The woman had a positive spin for everything that went wrong and a delightful sense of glee for everything that went right.

"Of course. But on the grand scheme of things, a little paint on an old shirt doesn't rate." She leaned forward and scratched at the kitty. "Isn't that true, little bit?"

Before he could react, the other kitten darted across the floor and began attacking the paint brush Dylan had set down to chase the first kitten. "Oh, brother."

"I'll get it." Rachel leapt over the miscellaneous items on the floor and grabbed for the kitten, slipping on a shim, arms and legs flailing like a cartoon comic strip, she slid across the obstacle course of his work area and splattered paint all over her clothes.

It hadn't been his plan, but the unexpected clown-like routine had Dylan chuckling out loud. "Sorry." Cradling the one kitten against his shoulder, he stretched an arm out to Rachel. "Let me help you up."

Sitting on her bottom and brushing her hands together quickly, a rush of pink filled her cheeks, for the first time all morning she wasn't smiling. "Thanks. I can get up on my own."

Biting on his lower lip, he bit back another laugh as she shifted about to push to her feet.

"Find something funny?" she asked as she straightened to her full height.

"Not at all." He placed the kitten back in the box. When he turned to face her, that bright smile was back, as well as an impish sparkle in her eyes. It took another moment to notice the paintbrush in her hand. "Uh-oh…"

Rachel had no idea what had come over her, but when she found her hand so close to the paint brush and heard Dylan laughing, she simply couldn't resist going after him.

"Now, Rachel." Dylan took a step in retreat.

"What?" Her words dripped with sugary innocence.

Dylan backed up till he bumped into the cat box. "You wouldn't want to get the cats covered in paint, would you?"

"Of course not." She stepped into his personal space. "They're not dressed."

Wide eyes filled with foreboding narrowed with confusion. "What?"

Her arm extending in front of her, she was all set to do a racing stripe down the front of his shirt when his hand snapped out and strong fingers strangled her wrist.

"I don't think you want to do that." He stood so close she could almost feel his heartbeat.

"I don't?" she teased in a weak effort to hide how her own heart rate was climbing. Then, bobbing her head, she sighed. "Okay. Maybe I don't."

Piercing hazel eyes stared at her a long moment before he also nodded and relinquished his hold on her. "We have work to do anyhow."

The second he stepped away from her, she quickly raised her arm. "Or maybe I do." Paint splattered across his chest. "Oops. Sorry."

"Oh. Just you wait." Dylan raised his arms like a charging bear.

Rachel took off running across the room, ducking behind a couple of new kitchen cabinets in the middle of the room waiting for installation. "Now, now. All is fair in love and war."

"And this is most definitely war."

"No." Her hands sprang up, palms out, as her head shook from side to side. "That's not what I meant." She bobbed left then right in an effort to avoid him. "Let's just call it even and get back to work."

"Not on your life." Whenever she dodged left, he leaned right. At this rate, they could be here all day.

"Really." She hesitated. "Time is money. Let's put down the paint brushes and get back to work." Dylan wasn't relenting. What had she gotten herself into? Another dodge left and she tripped over an unopened can of paint and went flying backwards, landing unceremoniously on her derriere.

Panic washed over Dylan's face. "Are you all right?" Still holding the paint brush, he hurried to where she lied flat on her back. "Is anything broken?"

"I don't know." Though she was pretty sure the only thing bruised was her ego.

Kneeling beside her, he set the brush down on the paper-covered floor. "Does anything hurt?"

Biting her lower lip, she read the sincere worry in his eyes and rather than appreciate the concern, she grabbed the brush with her free hand and swiped it across his chest again.

"You little stinker." Reaching for her wrist and the brush, he slipped and fell splat on top of her.

All she could think of was to swipe the brush again, but there was no way she was moving an inch with all six foot plus of man sprawled across her. A bubble of giggles erupted, growing louder until the two of them were laughing like a couple of hyenas, unable to move.

"Dylan Schaefer. What exactly are you doing to that poor woman?" Hands on her hips, elbows sticking out like chicken wings, a handsome woman in a blue dress frowned down at them.

"Oops." Dylan scrambled to his feet.

"Don't just stand there." The woman glared at him. "Help her up."

"Of course." A contrite expression took over his face as he extended a hand to Rachel. Lowering his voice, he leaned in. "Are you okay?"

She bobbed her head.

"Mom. This is my boss, Rachel. Rachel, my mom, Liz."

Now that she smiled, Rachel could see the family resemblance.

"Nice to meet you." The woman's gaze went from Rachel to her son. "I thought I taught you better."

"It was an accident, Mom." He reached for a rag nearby and handed it to Rachel.

"Thanks." She quickly wiped the droplets of paint that had made it to her face and handed the rag back to him.

As he wiped his face, he turned to his mother. "What are you doing here?"

"Your brother gave me the address. Said I had to see for myself what you're up to, or I wouldn't believe it. Since I live so close, here I am."

"Would you like me to show you around?" Rachel moved in closer.

"Thank you, that would be lovely."

She turned to Dylan. "Or would you prefer to show your mother around?"

"No." He shook his head. "I'm going to get a clean shirt out of my truck."

His lips pressed tightly together, his gaze was filled with concern of a different kind. Waiting a few moments until his mother began walking across the room, Dylan barely shook his head, then sighed and left the room.

Rachel's gaze darted from Dylan's back across to his mother crossing the large family room. It was nice that Dylan seemed so close to his mother, heaven knows Derek never talked about her. She needed to ask herself, why did she ever think the two brothers had anything in common besides their mother?

CHAPTER TEN

Ripping off the sloppy paint-covered shirt, Dylan tossed it into the back of his truck and pulled on an old t-shirt.

What the heck was his mom doing here? In all of his working career, the woman had never shown up to visit out of the blue. Of course, having a desk job in a major corporation was quite different than building cabinetry on a construction site. Still.

Inside, he could hear his mother and Rachel chatting. They were in the library.

"These high ceilings are amazing." Her hand running across the stripped wood, his mother glanced up. "And the crown molding is spectacular."

"That's what I thought." Rachel nodded. "I'm extremely blessed that your son was available to help with all this work."

"Yes." His mother frowned.

"Is something wrong?" Rachel asked.

"No. Not wrong." Still frowning, his mom faced her. "My son is the carpenter?"

"Yes, Mom. Remember, I took a leave of absence from my job."

For a moment his mother still looked confused before the light returned to her eyes and she nodded. "Oh, yes. That's right."

He resisted the overwhelming urge to sigh. No matter what his brother said, or thought, Dylan was convinced that his mother's memory was getting worse and her ability to cover up was getting better. He'd bet money that she didn't remember the conversation at all.

For the next little while, his mother walked through the house oohing and aahing over all the same details that made him love this old house. By the time they were done touring, he'd almost second-guessed himself about her memory. She seemed every bit the woman who raised him, admiring the craftsmanship of the original home, adding suggestions when Rachel detailed her plans, and teasing them over finding them sprawled out on the floor.

"If more employers and employees spent their workday tumbling about on the floor, maybe the unemployment rate wouldn't be so high," his mom said. When she winked at him and sidled up softly whispering, "I like her," he was reminded of almost the exact same reaction over his college girlfriend. Of course, his mother had been aching so long for grandchildren, she kept threatening to knit one.

The bright pink flush of Rachel's cheeks and the way her jaw dropped and her mouth moved but no words came out, almost had him scolding his mother. Still, it shouldn't have surprised him that before he could utter a word, that familiar smile took over Rachel's face, and grinning at his mother, she nodded. "You may have something there."

"I'd better be getting home. You remember my old friend Margaret Hess, she isn't feeling well and I want to make a King Ranch casserole for her. It's her favorite." His mom gave him a kiss on the cheek, and waved at Rachel as she hurried out the door.

"Well." Rachel sighed. "That was the most embarrassing moment of my life."

"I wish."

"Really?" Her grin brightened and her eyes sparkled with mischief. "Do tell?"

He chuckled and shook his head. "Not on your life." There were some things in his past that, like Vegas, were meant to stay in his past. Though oddly, something inside him actually wanted to tell her all about his past, every inch of it, and then he wanted to hear all about her. Not what he could find online, but the real her. From her first pet to her favorite color and foods. He wanted to know it all, and wasn't that an interesting new predicament for him?

Covered in paint from neck to knees, Rachel would have preferred to head home to shower and change before going to the ranch, but she was expected at six pm sharp, and with rush-hour traffic looming, she'd be unlikely to arrive by dessert, never mind dinner, if she stopped at home.

"Good heavens." Her grandmother stood in the front hall. "I'm guessing nobody told you that we apply paint with a brush or roller, not ourselves?" Only the smile on Lila Baron's face gave away the humor behind her words.

"It's complicated." Carefully, Rachel leaned over to kiss her grandmother on the cheek without getting any paint on her. Probability was at this point everything was already dry but it still felt moist against her skin so in her way of thinking, better safe than sorry.

Her sister Leah came down the stairs. "Complicated? That sounds like it involves a man."

So how did she answer this one. Yes, it involved a man, but not the way her sister thought. "If the carpenter counts, then yes. If you mean man as in significant other, no."

Studying her with one eye closed, Leah didn't move.

"Is the carpenter married?" Her cousin Eve's voice carried from across the foyer.

Was he? The few times, the very few times, Derek had mentioned his brother, there was never a mention of a wife. And in all the time Dylan and she had been working together, there wasn't any mention of a girlfriend, never mind a wife. She was almost embarrassed to admit that she didn't know the answer. At least not for sure. "What difference would that make? He's my carpenter, not a blind date."

Bouncing down the stairs as if she were still twelve years old, Rachel's cousin Siobhan slid to a halt by all the women now gathered in the middle of the foyer. "And why can't a carpenter be a date?"

This conversation was getting totally out of control. "I'm sure he'd be a lovely date for somebody. But all I want right now is to wash up for dinner so if y'all will excuse me, I'll be back in fifteen."

Her grandmother called after her, "Take twenty if you need it, supper isn't quite ready."

Opting not to bother drying her hair, Rachel was dressed and downstairs in just under twenty minutes. Despite the awkwardness of the conversation in the front hall, there was nothing she looked forward to better than a passel of family at her grandparents' home. She especially loved when her cousins were there at the same time. Her mom and dad traveled a lot now that they had retired, so she and her siblings gathered often at the ranch. Tonight was one of those nights when it felt like half the family was sprawled around the living room.

"What's this about a new man in your life?" Her brother Devlin finished pouring himself a drink. "Whoever he is, I sure hope he's better than the last idiot you dated."

Rachel had only brought Derek around to family events two or three times in the two years she dated him. There was always one reason or other why it wasn't convenient to blend their schedules, but after a while, she simply didn't want to bother. If she were willing to face facts, the truth was, deep down she knew her brother was right—Derek was an idiot. She cast a sideways glance at the women who had been with her in the foyer, and shaking her head rolled her eyes skyward. "There is no new man in my life. Dylan is my carpenter, not my love interest."

For whatever reason, the second the words left her mouth, she found herself remembering Dylan sprawled on top of her, laughing like they were the only two who knew the funniest joke in the world. Despite the mess, the wet paint, and his mom walking in on them, that silly incident was the most fun she had with a man in a very long time.

"I'm guessing if he's working for you, he's good at what he does." Eve's comment was more of a statement than a question.

"Of course he is." Leah rolled her eyes at their cousin. "Why would she work with anyone who wasn't good? He's probably better than good, right?" Leah turned to her.

She had to nod. He was indeed better than good.

"Carpentry can be an art." Siobhan lifted her glass. "Bet he's good with his hands." Over the rim of her drinking glass, Siobhan glanced up at Rachel. A sly grin teased at the corners of her mouth, her gaze darted to her grandmother and grandfather before settling back on Rachel. Her voice lowered to just above a whisper. "You know, there's much to be said about a man who's good with his hands."

Almost choking on her drink, Rachel spewed ice water like a poolside fountain. Maybe joining the whole family for supper wasn't the best idea she'd ever had.

CHAPTER ELEVEN

Unable to sleep, Dylan gave up on the idea and instead, filled his mug with coffee and headed early to the house. They'd lost a bit of time yesterday horsing around with the paint and showing his mother around. He wanted to catch up. He also had a few ideas he wanted to work through to share with Rachel. He had no idea if she wanted his input or not, but the longer he worked on this project, the more invested he was. Most of the time the house felt not like his job, but like his baby.

His former job did have a tremendous amount of satisfaction, and gave him a very hefty bank account. Still, the joy of creating something with his own hands and then seeing the pleasure it brought to other people was a very different sense of satisfaction. After all, just how much money did a single man need in the bank?

Closing the door of his truck, he juggled the keys, the cup, and his ringing phone. "Whatever it is, the answer is no."

Derek's low chuckle came through the phone line. "Is that any way to talk to your baby brother?"

"Sorry. Good morning. How are you?"

"Doing great, but I want to talk to you about something."

"Sure. And no." Fumbling with the keys, he undid the latch and turned the knob, shoving the back door open, momentarily surprised to hear a sound from the other side of the house.

"You're going to have to get a new repertoire. I'm not asking for money. I do have a job."

Not that holding down a job ever stopped his brother

from borrowing money. He pretty much held a job his entire adult life. The problem was what he spent his money on, and how much of it he spent, and the tendency to fall off the face of the earth without notice or explanation regardless of how important it was for him to participate—like supporting him during Jim's funeral. Derek's world always came first. Now that Dylan knew his brother had been dating a wealthy member of the Baron family, it explained why the guy was always broke. No doubt he was trying to keep up with the Joneses and failing miserably. Or more precisely, keeping up with the Barons. "To what do I owe the pleasure of this conversation?"

"Mom tells me that you're doing really well on the project with Rachel."

"Mom told you that, did she?" Taking his time, he slowly made his way toward where he thought he'd heard movement near the master bedroom. Julio and his crew were working on painting the walls, but he hadn't expected any of them here this early.

"Mom has been Chatty Cathy lately. I don't know why, but she seems happier, less restless. I'm not sure if it's because she's been playing cards again with her friends, or if it's because she got to see you at work."

With no sign of workers for anyone else in the back bedroom, Dylan shook his head. Now he was hearing things. "Or maybe Mom was happy you took her out to lunch last week. You know how much she loves her baby boy, even if you are over thirty."

"Nah. I think it's the meds she's taking. She seems like her old self."

Some of the time. The truth was, meds or no meds, some days, confusion just made itself at home in her head. "I'm a little worried about her. When she showed up here unexpectedly, she seemed really confused at some moments. Especially when I reminded her I was working with carpentry right now."

A moment of silence hung, he could almost hear his brother thinking. "She's getting older, you have to expect her to forget a few things. I'm sure even you forget where you leave your car keys from time to time."

Even though his brother couldn't see him, Dylan shook his head. "This is different. Most of the time, Mom is Mom. By the end of her visit, she was having a great time sharing design ideas with Rachel. But when she was confused, her eyes went blank. There was nobody home for those few moments. I'm worried she shouldn't be living alone anymore."

"I think you're just borrowing trouble. You're always the worry wart – always Debbie Downer – work, work, work, and expect the worst. It'll take years for this disease to run its course. Mom is fine. Let her enjoy this time in her own home with her friends. And speaking of Rachel, how's that going?"

Just like Derek to ignore something he didn't like. Yes, their mom had friends, but even they'd noticed her recent challenges with her memory. His mother was probably going to have to be sitting in a corner staring into space before Derek would admit that she had something wrong with her. Even now, it had taken way too long to convince his kid brother that their mother needed neurological testing for her memory. Thankfully, so far, she was still capable of taking her meds on her own. Even if she thought they were vitamins. But he wasn't fooling himself, he knew one of these days, she was going to need a lot more help. As for Rachel, that was none of his brother's business. "Rachel is a good boss and has a great design eye."

"That's not all that's great about Rachel."

"Look, man. I really have to get to work." He refused to talk about Rachel with his brother. Whatever their relationship had been, he didn't want to know anything about it. Nor did he want to share anything now with Derek. "We'll talk later about Mom."

The heavy sigh carried through the phone. "Fine. But I'm telling you, stop borrowing trouble. Mom is fine."

Some days, he wished he could be as cavalier about life as Derek; then again, it was probably that same attitude that had Rachel kicking Derek's sorry butt to the curb. More than once he'd wondered how or why his brother would let a woman like that get away. Each time it came down to the same thing: Derek had to be the biggest idiot on the planet.

Some days were just too good to be true. Yesterday the inspector had come by for the next phase of the rehab, and they had passed with flying colors. Just one more deadline and she'd be finished with the annoying inspections. Since all was on schedule, rather than start her morning out at the house, she decided to check out a few of her favorite haunts for finding special pieces. Right now she was so excited, she could dance a jig.

Keys in hand, she hopped out of the truck and hurried to the front door. Things were finally looking like the images she had all this time in her head. She just loved bringing old houses back to life. And this old house was definitely proving to be her favorite.

Entering through the kitchen door, the sounds of tools buzzing and humming throughout the house was music to her ears. Hurrying across the room, she paused briefly to chat with Julio, gave a couple of minor instructions to others in the crew, and then found Dylan in the library. "Yoo hoo."

"Hey." Dylan turned off his sander. "Didn't think you were coming by today."

"Was out sourcing a few items. I could use some help if this can wait."

Dylan bobbed his head. "Sure. I'm all yours."

Heat suddenly rushed up her system at the double entendre and settled in her cheeks. Thank heaven she didn't have the same paper white complexion her sister Leah had. "I found a piece I want for the dining room at the Wrecking Yard."

"The where?" Dylan could not have looked more surprised if she told him she found a piece she liked in the bowels of hell.

"Wrecking Yard. It's a salvage company. I find all sorts

of fun things there, though the owner is out of town this week and his pregnant wife is minding the store."

"Okay." Dylan nodded, placing his sander in the lockable tool chest.

"I need help loading the pieces."

"You want to use my truck?"

She shook her head. "I brought one of the trucks from the ranch. What I need from you is brute strength."

"Well, I suppose it could be worse." He cracked a smile. "You could have said you wanted me for my mind."

That had her laughing out loud. They quipped back and forth for a bit on their way out the door and then the ride over to the Wrecking Yard the conversation switched to his mother.

"It's sweet the way you worry about her." Rachel took the exit off the freeway. "They say it's part of the circle of life. Your parents take care of you, and then one day, you're taking care of your parents. At least there are five of us. There are only two of you. And no offense, but I don't picture Derek being much help."

"He loves our mother. He's just not ready to accept that she's changing."

"I suspect there are a lot of things he's not willing to accept." She stole a moment to glance at his direction. "In all the time we dated, he only mentioned your mom once. He might have mentioned you twice. The Math Guru, that's what he called you. I thought you were a professor or actuary until the next time you came up and he mentioned you were in finance. I realize now he wasn't annoyed with you, he was jealous."

"Jealous?"

She bobbed her head. "You got your MBA and he doesn't like school."

"It's not that he doesn't like it exactly, it was just difficult. Did you know he's dyslexic?"

Frowning she shook her head. How had she missed that?

"He struggled to keep up in school. Covered up by perfecting the art of socializing. It's actually a shame. In many ways, I believe he's smarter than me, but he just couldn't master academia. I suspect that fueled the part of his personality that if it doesn't come easily, then he's not going to do it at all. Unfortunately, relationships aren't easy." Silence hung for a long moment before he leaned against the window. "So why, uh, did you two break up?"

Wasn't that a loaded question. "I suppose the easy answer is, I smartened up. No offense, but your brother's an idiot."

He chuckled. "No offense taken."

When he didn't say anything else, she knew he was waiting for the rest of the story. "The first year, your brother did a great job of hiding his flaws. He was smart, friendly, and always made me smile. But then the cracks started to appear in the façade. Things seemed to evolve more around him and less around us. What he wanted to eat, what movie he wanted to see, and there was a growing tendency to forget his wallet in his other pants, or on the dresser, or in Timbuktu for all I knew. Eventually I figured out my money was way more important than me."

"I'm sorry."

She shrugged. "It took me longer than it should have to admit that I'd wasted a lot of time on a loser, but when it finally struck me that I deserved more than he was willing to contribute, I broke it off."

"You're right about one thing."

"Only one?" she teased.

"You're worth a great deal." He chuckled. "And my brother is an idiot."

"Are you as good a brother as you are a son?"

"Both those points are debatable."

"I don't know about Derek. But you are definitely a good son."

His head tipped to one side. "That's nice of you to say."

She shook her head. "Just stating facts. I've heard you talk to her on the phone, watched how you interacted with her, and see how worried you are now. You're a good guy, Dylan Schaefer." A really good guy.

CHAPTER TWELVE

Many things crossed Dylan's mind as they wound their way to the salvage shop. Maybe someday his brother would mature into the man he could be, but Dylan also knew that day was a long way off.

"And here we are." Rachel pulled into a parking space and sprang out of the car. Habit had him darting slightly ahead of her and holding open the door. From the brief sideways glance she cast in his direction, Dylan had the feeling that holding the door for a lady was one habit his mother had drummed into both of them, but his brother had not kept up.

"Afternoon, Miss Baron." From behind a nearby counter, a woman about the same age as Rachel smiled at her.

The way the woman shifted, it was obvious she was about to climb off a stool and Rachel waved her off. "Don't get up on my account. I know where the piece is."

The lady nodded and eased back down. "Works for me. Getting around is getting harder and harder and I still have over a month to go."

"It'll be here before you know it," Rachel encouraged her.

The place did indeed look like an indoor junkyard, although, on closer inspection, he could see more than one treasure buried under layers, or perhaps years, of accumulated dust. Having passed through one large room and out into an even larger room akin to a warehouse with every possible architectural feature of older homes, he happened to glance up. Chandeliers of every size, shape, and design hung from every inch of the ceiling. "Wow."

Rachel paused and following his gaze, looked up and smiled at him. "Fun, isn't it?"

"Very." He could feel his cheeks tugging at the corners of his mouth. "This place is amazing."

"Watch your step!" Her arm shot straight out in front of him, a practiced move from a mom of a long-gone era.

Immediately stopping in place, waving his arms to catch his balance, he glanced down and realized he teetered over a huge, rusty, old-fashioned tub. "That was a close call."

"Yeah. You gotta watch where you're going. It's too easy to be distracted."

He nodded and walked more closely behind her.

"There it is." Against a far wall, her finger pointed to a massive, hand-carved … something. "What is it, exactly?"

"Beautiful." Her smile spreading from ear to ear, she happily rocked on the balls of her feet. "It's going to look great in the dining room, except…" She blew out a heavy sigh and her smile slipped just a smidge. "We'll need to do several modifications to make it fit the space."

With every word out of her mouth, his head continued to bob. She was absolutely correct. The piece was stunning and massive and created by a person very proud of their craft. "What did you have in mind?"

She proceeded to explain her vision. Separating the two pieces. Shortening the mirrored hutch portion of the piece, and finally she showed him portions that were damaged. "We'll have to cut this off, try to balance the pieces. Hopefully no one will have any idea what they're missing."

He leaned forward and ran his hand along the tattered section, then squatting down, eased closer. "I think I can match this."

"You do?" If her eyes were any wider, she'd qualify for a Halloween decoration.

"Don't look so surprised."

"Sorry." She blinked. "That would be great."

"Then let's get it to my place."

"Your place?"

"Is there an echo in here?" He plastered on the best smile he could muster. Though, the more time he spent with

Rachel, the easier that smile came.

"Why your place?"

"I have a shop in my garage. It will be easier to work on the piece there, then when it's finished we can carefully transport it to the house. Some of the final details will have to be touched up in place, but the majority of work I can do in my garage."

She nodded. "Makes sense."

Together, with the help of a furniture dolly, they managed to move the heavy buffet out to the parking lot. Working their way back inside to inform the owner they were done, he grabbed hold of her arm. "Did you see that?"

Her head whipped around and her gaze followed the direction his finger was pointing. "Which that?"

"The over mantle."

She leaned in and he knew the second she spotted the piece he was referring to. Not only did her eyes light up like the Fourth of July skies, that smile he'd grown so fond of bloomed just as bright. "How did I miss that?"

"It would be great for the fireplace in the formal living room."

Her head bobbed. "Yep."

It was rather silly, but he was extremely delighted to contribute to the design side of the job.

"I'll go tell Julie. You go rustle up that dolly again."

A little later, they had everything loaded in the car and were boogying down the freeway, chatting about everything and anything related to the project, and he was loving every minute of it. Had he ever had so much fun talking woodwork and antiques with a woman before? Something told him, if he wanted to talk stocks and ETFs, she'd keep up just the same. No matter how he looked at it, this woman was simply amazing.

When Dylan said he had a workshop, he wasn't kidding. Every kind of saw, sander, and chisel imaginable was neatly stored or displayed along with counter space galore for working with. "This is too cool."

As she stood over a large metal contraption with a plastic bubble, she had to ask, "What's this?"

"It's for sucking up sawdust. Otherwise things can get crazy in here. Especially if I'm staining a finished piece."

"Of course."

They settled all the pieces into a vacant area most likely left that way for this very purpose, storing projects.

They gave the over mantle a last shove into place and her stomach growled, loudly. "Sorry. I may have skipped lunch."

From the frown that formed between his brows, anyone would think she'd just kicked his dog. "You should have said something. We could have done drive thru."

She shrugged. "I'll grab a bite when I get home later."

"Come on." He waved for her to follow him. "I can probably rustle something up quickly to keep you going till you drop me back at the house to get my car and go on your merry way."

"You don't have to do that."

"I don't have to, but I'm going to."

How could she resist that smile? He was quite sparing with them. Too bad the wattage of his grin could make a woman weak in the knees. If she were interested, that is. And of course she wasn't. Was she?

"Have a seat." He gestured to the kitchen table, and two little fur balls waddled into the room, meowing.

"You'd think I never fed them." Leaning over to pick one up and single-handedly snuggle it against him, he pulled out a bag and filled a dish near the fridge with food. Then he rubbed the kitten's back and set it down by the bowl.

"Haven't found them a home yet?"

He shrugged.

Her own smile widened. "You're going to keep them, aren't you?"

Again, he shrugged, grabbing ingredients. "Maybe."

She couldn't help chuckling. "You really are surprising."

"Oh, how so?"

"For a bachelor, you have a great way with little animals and you also have a great kitchen."

"They're kittens, doesn't take much effort to feed and water them. And as for my kitchen, it's a kitchen." He closed the under-stove cabinet and set a frying pan on the cook top.

"You don't actually have to cook."

"I'm not."

"Could have fooled me. What else do you do with a frying pan?"

"Fried bologna sandwiches, of course."

"Of course." She watched him butter the pan, pull out the bread, and to her surprise, bologna. "You're not kidding."

"Why would I kid about fried bologna sandwiches?"

She didn't consider herself a food snob by any means, but she really didn't think anyone too young for a retirement community even knew what a fried bologna sandwich was, never mind actually eat one. It took everything in her not to cringe as he flipped the bologna and then splattered layers of mayo on toast. The next thing she knew, she had a sandwich on a paper plate with potato chips in front of her.

"Try it. I promise you won't die."

Hoping her smile didn't look like a grimace, she nodded and gingerly picked up the sandwich.

"It's not going to explode or bite you." Now he was chuckling at her.

Still trying to smile, she took a bite—and almost died. "Oh, my heavens. This is amazing."

"Told you."

Not till she had practically inhaled the sandwich did she realize just how hungry she'd been. "I can't believe I've gone my entire life without ever eating one of these sandwiches, and I especially am surprised to learn you are indeed a man of many talents. Remind me never to underestimate you again."

"If you like my fried bologna sandwich, you'll love my

roast beef sandwich."

"Let's see. Meatloaf, bologna and now, leftover roast beef. Just to confirm, as in you cook it in the oven, or are we talking bought a gourmet grocery store?"

He shook his head. "I thought you said you were never going to underestimate?"

Oh did she have a lot to learn about this man, and she was pretty sure she was going to love the ride.

CHAPTER THIRTEEN

Who knew cooking for a woman could be this much fun. Not that most people would consider a sandwich cooking. His mind had wandered to the point that he lost track of what she was talking about.

"Yoo hoo." Rachel waved a potato chip in front of him. "Was I that boring?"

"Boring? Never. I was merely momentarily distracted. Please continue." He reached over to grab one of the chips on her plate, delighted when rather than make a snarky remark, she nudged the dish closer to him.

"Thank you."

"You have a lot to offer a lucky woman."

Okay, whatever she was saying, he hadn't thought that was it.

That made him chuckle. "Not many agree with you."

"Why is that?"

Did he really want to get into his life story? Now? Here? With her? "It's a long story."

"I've got time."

"It's hard to devote yourself to one woman when you're married to your job." Apparently, he was indeed going to bare his soul here and now.

Her only reaction was a raised eyebrow.

"As you know, I used to be in finance. Nothing as simple as a book-keeper or even as busy as an accountant in tax season. My career was eighty to hundred and twenty hours a week, gallons of coffee, and enough stress to crush a lump of coal into a diamond."

"Doesn't sound like an ideal lifestyle."

"It paid for this." He waved his arm at the walls around

them and toward the back door and garage beyond. "Not only is this house fully paid for but all that equipment that I hardly ever had time to use is also free and clear."

"Hardly ever?"

He shrugged. "Okay, not at all until recently."

Her head nodded slowly, her gaze drifted over his shoulder to the back door and then settled once again on him. "What happened recently?"

Just thinking about Jim squeezed at his chest like one of the wood clamps in his workshop. "One of my best friends, Jim, worked as hard as I did. We occasionally kicked back a beer in celebration of some fiscal triumph or other, but usually we burned the midnight oil together. Some would say we burned the candle at both ends."

Rachel nodded, but remained silent.

"He was only thirty-nine. One morning, he didn't show up at the office, didn't call, and didn't answer his phone." Dylan paused a moment to take a deep breath, not really surprised how much it all still hurt. "Jim always answered his phone. We used to joke that the guy could be making love with Miss America and stop to answer his phone. It was discussed to wait till noon, but my boss made the call to the police for a wellness check. Jim was slumped at his desk in his home office. He'd had a heart attack. He'd been gone for hours."

"I'm sorry."

"Seeing how someone whose life so easily paralleled mine could be here one minute and gone the next hit me hard. Harder than I would have imagined. For the first time in a long time, I stopped and took a long hard look at my life and where I was going. It suddenly struck me that what did it matter how much money I had if there was no time to spend it."

"I can certainly attest that money does not guarantee happiness." Quite unexpectedly, her hand reached out and settled on his. "Look at my cousin Mitch, or Uncle Doug. All the money in Texas couldn't save their wives or take away the hurt from the loss. And look at my uncle Bradley. He's on wife number four. I don't know that he's ever been truly happy, though maybe, since this wife seems to be sticking, he's happier."

Dylan couldn't peel his gaze away from her hand on his. A comforting warmth seemed to rush up his arm and spread through every cell in his body.

"So, are you thinking of going back to the office at some point?"

He shook his head. For weeks now he'd been asking himself the same thing. Suddenly, as clear as day, looking into her deep green eyes and the honest concern glistening behind them, he knew that he may not always be a carpenter, but he was never going to go back to that time in his life again. "No. It looks like, at least for now, you're stuck with me."

Leaning back, she smiled. "If that's the case, there's a house on Cedar Ridge that I've been eyeing."

"The next project?"

"Maybe." Her grin broadened, and then her gaze shifted to the kitchen window. "Oh my, it's dark out. I'd better get you back to your truck and make sure the crew locked everything up."

Simply because of how much he really did not want to leave and then come back to an empty house, he knew that leaving now was indeed a very good idea. "Let's go then."

The mood in the short ride to Hartwig House was considerably lighter than the conversation at the table. He'd shared a couple of stories from growing up and going to college, and even shared the one real vacation he'd taken to Thailand with a woman he'd been dating. Her blonde hair and blue eyes had been like a magnet for the locals and he'd spent more time photographing her with the locals when they handed him their cameras than he had of the country. At the time he'd been pretty annoyed; retelling it now, they'd both had a good laugh. "Seriously," he shook his head, "you'd think she was a green alien from an episode of *Star Trek* the way they all reacted."

"Any idea what happened to her?"

"Actually," he rolled his eyes skyward, "she met a guy from Paraguay our last week and decided to stay. I think they have two or three kids now."

"Dodged that bullet."

"Maybe." The thought of having a couple of kids hadn't been in the forefront of his mind, but if anyone were to ask him right this minute, with Rachel, if he'd like to have kids some day, the answer would be a most resounding yes, and wasn't that just one more twist in the craziness called his life?

Rachel pulled into the driveway and blew out a sigh. "Whoever left last forgot to turn off the light in the master."

"I'll turn it all off and lock up before I head back home." He'd been out his door and already circled the hood to get Rachel's door for her.

Oh, how she loved the way he did all the things her grandfather did for her grandmother and her dad for her mom. Grams had always said a good man will cherish you every day in little ways. Dylan's ways were growing on her. "Have I mentioned how much I like that you're not letting Texas Chivalry die?"

"You have now." Not for the first time in the last few days, his smile was wide and his eyes bright.

She could easily get used to seeing that smile more often. If she were honest with herself, she'd already gotten used to seeing that smiling face every day. She didn't like the idea of how empty her days would feel if he didn't join her on the next project. But right now, she had a house to lock up; she could ponder her lonely future another day. "Thank you, but the house is my responsibility. I'll do a walk through."

He nodded. "Fine, but I'll follow. Want to see that no one messed with my work while I was gone."

"Fair enough." Somehow she doubted that he was really worried about his work and suspected it was more of that sense of chivalry rearing its head. Either way, she nodded and led the way to the back door, turned the knob and sighed again. "Of course, no one locked it."

Inside, the soft sound of music barely reached the kitchen. Dylan's smile slipped and his gaze narrowed. "Maybe someone's working late?"

With a shrug and a good dose of confusion, Rachel slipped her keys into her pocket and started for the master, so intent on her destination she almost did a face plant over a five-gallon bucket of paint. Knocking over the broom and wooden pole resting against it, she stumbled about to regain her balance, making enough noise to raise the dead while she was at it. "Oops."

"Easy there." Dylan grabbed her arm until he was sure she was steady on her feet.

"Why the heck is that in the middle of the room anyhow?" She glanced at the pile of painter's supplies, then up at him. Not till this split second did she realize how close to her he was standing, or how good he smelled. Was that his cologne? Soap? Or just him?

Still holding on to her, his gaze darkened and his voice fell to a near whisper. "I'm, uh, guessing they didn't… think we were coming back."

"No," she shook her head, her gaze locked on his lips, "I guess not."

"I, uh, shouldn't do this, but…" His mouth came crashing down on hers and every nerve ending in her entire body sprang to life.

Man, oh, man, could Dylan Schaefer kiss. His strong hands still delicately held her in place against him. And heaven help her, she hoped he never let go. Until a clatter and clank, much like what Rachel had just done falling over the painting tools, sounded from the master and she realized the music was no longer playing. The sound had clearly startled Dylan as well since he released his hold and took a step in retreat. To her his expression looked as dazed as she felt.

Gathering her wits, another clatter came from the room and she spun on her heels as ready as possible to deal with the source of the noise.

Dylan reached out and grabbed her arm. "Hang on

there." His expression had darkened. "Let me look first."

"Not on your life." Rachel patted the belly band on her stomach. "I've got your back."

One eyebrow shot up as his gaze darted from her hand back to her face. Not the kiss-dazed look of a moment before, but one of disapproval.

"Don't look at me like that. I've got a permit and I can shoot the tin can off a tree limb halfway to Dallas. You don't grow up on a Texas ranch, even in the summers, without knowing how to shoot straight. Let's go. It's probably just a raccoon or stray cat looking for food. Maybe even mama cat looking for her kittens."

The way his face momentarily contorted, she knew he didn't think that for a second. She sure hoped he was wrong. At the bedroom door, Dylan raised his finger to his lips, then wrapped the other hand around the knob and slowly turned it, pushing the door open just in time to see a booted foot go through the window.

"Oh my God!" she shouted, hurrying over to the open window and sticking her head out before turning to follow after Dylan through the house, and out the back door.

The intruder had a bag over his shoulder, making him look like a homeless Santa Claus, and long legs that carried him across the backyard and into the alley before she or Dylan could come even close to catching up. In the alley, there was no sign of the person.

"Must have cut through a neighbor's yard." Dylan had his phone out and dialed 911 as he walked back into the house.

While he spoke with the police, she looked around the empty room. Empty bags from a local burger joint were on the floor. In the corner of the room, a five-dollar bill sat crumpled beside another bag with an apple and two bananas. Suddenly Rachel's fury over someone invading her project house slithered away at the thought that this person may have lost their last five dollars and only food they could have for days. So on top of everything else she had to deal with, what was she going to do about this new wrinkle?

CHAPTER FOURTEEN

Now the few oddities Dylan had noticed over the last couple of weeks made sense. The missing food, the moved items—all of it had been the intruder. From what he could see, the person was using the master bedroom for a hotel room. What Dylan didn't understand was how were they getting inside? He or Rachel were usually the last to leave and the doors were always locked, as well as all the windows.

Being a construction zone, there was a lock box on the back door in case he or Rachel wasn't there and a contractor needed access. Could it be a homeless contractor? Last night he'd stayed on-site while the police came in search of prints. A few smudged prints were left on the sill of the window Dylan and Rachel had watched the person climb out of. The person must have been alerted to their presence when Rachel went tumbling over the paint container. The intruder had a few moments to gather their belongings—he was guessing whatever was in that bag—and run for the proverbial hills.

Maybe tonight he would stay and keep an eye out.

"Morning." Rachel breezed into the house. As usual, her smile was bright and not a soul would guess from her pleasant demeanor that she'd had the bejesus scared out of her last night by a vagrant.

On the other hand, he had just enough male ego to wonder if he had something to do with that smile. Heaven knew he had a heck of a time getting any sleep last night. He told himself it was the uncomfortable sleeping conditions, or that it was the concern over everyone's safety because of the intruder, but the truth was Rachel was the reason he couldn't sleep. Nothing could stop him from thinking about that too short and too-sweet kiss. "Morning."

"Anything new on our guest?"

"Guest?" Only Rachel would come up with that. "Not that I know of. Have the police contacted you?"

She huffed out a sigh. "Apparently, mine are the only viable prints on the sill. I must have smudged the other prints when I leaned against it to see where the person went."

In such a hurry to chase the person down, it hadn't occurred to him to remind Rachel to stay away from the window. Anyone who had ever read a good mystery book knew that. "Just in case, I picked up some new locks and will change them out in a bit."

"Good idea. Don't forget to change out the lock box key."

"About that."

"Yes?"

"In case it's a contractor who already has the code, it might be a good idea to change the code. Perhaps hold off giving it out to anyone you don't know well."

Her head bobbed. "Good idea." Her lips pulled into a thin line she shook her head. "Do you really think one of my regular contractors could be in trouble?"

"There's only one way to find out. Ask them, but if someone says yes, what will you do?"

"Help." Her nose crinkled in thought. "I just have to figure out how without bruising any relationships. Or egos."

"You really care, don't you?"

"Of course I do." Why that surprised him, he didn't know. Too many years working with too many people who put profit and the almighty dollar first had tainted his perspective on all that was good and decent in this world.

"Yoo hoo." A woman's voice carried from the kitchen. A familiar voice.

"Mom?" He stepped away from Rachel and walked toward where his mother stood in the middle of the empty kitchen. "What are you doing here?"

"I love this neighborhood. Everyone is so friendly and

the trees are probably a hundred years old. It's so shady for an afternoon walk, and so quiet for an evening walk."

"Evening walk? Mom, what are you talking about?"

"Nothing." His mom shook her head. "Where's Mary? I brought her some of my French toast casserole."

"Mary?" Now he was the one confused. "Who's Mary?"

"Why, she owns this old place."

Standing in front of them with a covered casserole dish in her hand and sporting a sweetly innocent smile, Dylan's mother reminded Rachel of a mom from a 1950s sitcom. Like Dylan, though, Rachel was completely confused over who the woman was talking about. "I'm the owner of this house."

The smile on Mrs. Alexander's face momentarily slipped. A dullness took over her gaze for a long moment before the light returned to her eyes along with her smile. "No, dear. Not you. Mary."

"Mary?" Dylan repeated.

"Yes. Nice young lady. About my height. Very sweet. I met her the first time, on my walk one night. Poor thing was locked out and had to climb in through the window."

"Window?" Rachel turned to Dylan, alarm bells going off in her head like a five-alarm fire at a station house.

"Excuse me, Mom." Dylan turned and strode quickly across the house, into the master bedroom, turned the window locks and then one by one, lifted each window. Sure enough, the mechanism of the window the intruder had climbed out of last night was turned in the locked position but doing nothing.

"That's how the person got in," Rachel softly uttered.

Lips pressed tightly together, Dylan nodded.

She knew exactly what he was thinking. Rachel had seen her fair share of homeless on the streets, too many suffered from mental illness and were considered a danger to themselves and others. What if this woman fell into that category? Mrs. Alexander could have been hurt, or worse. Even though she wasn't Rachel's mother, her blood pressure shot up and her heart took off at a rapid clip. "We have to find her."

"Mary or the intruder?" His eyes rounded and his brows rose.

"Both. Especially if they're one and the same. Even if we fix the lock on the window and it turns out they are indeed the same person, what's to say she won't go looking for your mother? If she's mentally unstable, she could fixate on an easy target, like an easily confused woman."

Those lips pressed tightly together as he nodded. "I've been telling Derek we need to install cameras at Mom's, make sure she's not struggling more than we think. But we've both been hesitant to invade Mom's privacy."

"Understandable."

"Still. Under the circumstances, I think it's time. Especially since we have no idea if this Mary person knows where Mom lives."

"Hopefully not. How far does your mom live from here?"

"Next neighborhood over. Maybe a fifteen minute walk."

Rachel frowned. "Too close for comfort."

"That's what I'm thinking. After work, I'm picking up those cameras."

"Why don't you go now? This is important."

He shook his head. "We're expecting the inspectors today. Last hurdle is the new panel box. I'm sure it will be good to go, but I don't want to risk not being here."

"I can stay."

"Yes, but I still would like to be here." He smiled. "If I'm going to continue in construction, it won't hurt to make nice with the inspectors."

"True." She found her mind shifting from worry about his mother to an overwhelming urge to lean in and kiss those smiling lips. It had taken everything in her to walk in the door this morning and act as if that all too brief kiss yesterday hadn't completely turned her insides to mush.

She must have been lost in thought longer than she'd realized. While her mind was still considering how such a short, sweet kiss could be so toe-tingling, the warmth of Dylan's hand settled on her arm and the low timbre of his voice pulled her back to the here and now. "Hey. You okay?"

Until he touched her, she was doing just fine. The only problem was that the heat of his touch had sent her brain into muddled mode. There was no way words would come. Her second challenge appeared when her silence drew him closer. So close, she could feel the tension of concern coming off him in waves.

"Rachel?"

That was it. His voice so close to her had her scrambled brain shutting down all filters of common sense and reasonable behavior for an employer and employee relationship. All her brain knew at this moment was that she was a woman, he was a man, and oh how she wanted to repeat last night's kiss. Closing the distance between them in a single step, she inched up on her tippy toes and pressed her lips to his.

Just as they had last night, sparks flew and her insides melted from the heat of his kiss. All she could think was that for her entire adult life, she'd definitely kissed all the wrong men.

The sound of heels clacking on the new floors was followed by a loud and sweet, "Yoo hoo," just like a short while ago had her springing away from Dylan.

The stunned look on his face quickly replaced with a wide grin. "And good morning to you too."

"There you are." Still holding the casserole dish, his mother walked into the bedroom. "Oh, I love the colors you chose. The white isn't quite white, is it?"

Rachel shook her head. "Just a shade off. It's softer that way."

"I like it. A lot." His mother slowly turned, taking in the room before facing her son. "If Mary's not home, can I just leave the casserole in the fridge?"

"There is no fridge." Dylan blew out a sigh. "Mom, let me take you and the casserole back to your house, then we'll sit down and have a nice chat about Mary."

"She's nice. I like her. As a matter of fact," his mom's smile turned impish, and she turned to fully face him, "you might like her too."

"Mom." Dylan eased closer to Rachel and gingerly, standing at her side, took hold of her hand. "I like Rachel."

His mother's brows curled a moment before her smile bounced back. "Well, that's nice. I like you too. But I still want Mary to have the casserole. Hopefully she'll be home soon." And without another word, his mother turned and walked back to the kitchen.

"So, you like me, huh?" Rachel teased.

He turned to face her and took both her hands in his. "You can't tell?"

"Well, I had maybe hoped."

"Hope away, because you may be stuck with me."

"There are worst things in life," she chuckled. "But your mom is waiting and the inspector is coming, and I want to find this Mary person. Find out what's going on."

He leaned forward, kissed the tip of her nose, and leaned back. "I'll hurry. I don't want to miss the inspector."

"Don't worry if your mom needs you." She really didn't want to let go of his hand.

"It'll be fine. And maybe I'll find out what the heck is going on."

There was an idea. Right about now she was just as curious as to what was going on with his mother and the intruder as she was about what was going on between them. The latter holding a lot more interest right now. She sure hoped she knew what she was getting into.

CHAPTER FIFTEEN

"**I** figured if anyone would have insight into what to do, it would be you, Governor." Rachel reached for another piece of Hazel's garlic toast. The cook's version of Texas Toast was the absolute best Rachel had ever eaten, anywhere. The inspector had come right after Dylan returned from dropping his mother off and Rachel decided even though the ranch was a bit of a drive, enjoying lunch with the entire family might get her some answers that weren't available to the general public.

"I wish I had an easy answer for you, but the homeless is a complex situation in today's society." The Governor shook his head at his granddaughter.

"If you can find out who he or she is, I'm a member of many organizations that want to help the homeless." Her grandmother sighed. "If you're sure it's a woman, there are a couple of places that focus on helping women. One will help her with living situations, another can help her get equipped for better jobs. There's even money available for continued education if the person is willing."

"The problem," the Governor waved a fork at his wife, "is that too many homeless aren't merely hard luck cases, they have severe mental health issues."

"Or worse," her brother Devlin spoke up, "PTSD. When I think of how hard it is for some veterans to get the care and treatment they need, it makes me want to punch the wall."

"Agreed." The Governor nodded. "The bigger the bureaucracy, the slower the wheels turn."

"So, what I'm hearing is that I need to find out what her story is before I can do much else?"

Heads bobbed around the table.

"From what Dylan shared about his conversation with his mother, the intruder sounds like just an average lady in a nice house with a nice smile."

"That's what his mother said?" Grams asked.

"Not exactly, she just spoke about her the way she would any neighbor. His mom has early stages of dementia. Sometimes she's totally with it, and sometimes she's a bit confused. Just our luck, this woman is one of his mother's confused moments."

"I agree with Dylan." Leah set her fork on her dish. "Cameras at his mother's house is a good idea. Not a bad one for your project house either. From a legal point of view, the old cliché an ounce of prevention is worth a pound of cure can come in very handy."

"Free legal advice, sis?" Devlin teased.

Laughing, Leah stuck her tongue out at her older brother. "Don't worry, I'll send her a bill."

"I can't afford you," Rachel laughed back.

"Sure you can." Leah smiled. "I'm thinking a dinner at my favorite steak house."

"Somehow," Devlin raised one brow at his legal eagle sister, "I don't think a cliché warrants a steak dinner. Now, if you were to truly help her…"

"Keep me posted on all of this and we'll see what we can do, okay?" Leah set her knife and fork side by side and pushed her chair away from the table. "Sorry to eat and run, but I have a 3 p.m. appointment with a new client and don't want to risk getting caught in traffic." She walked around the table, kissing both her grandparents goodbye, and then bolted for the foyer.

"I suppose," Rachel did the same with her silverware, set her napkin on the table and stood, "I should get going too. I'll let y'all know what happens next."

"You be careful, dear." Her grandmother smiled at her and her grandfather nodded his agreement.

"I will. I promise." Being careful wasn't a concern. Getting to the bottom of who the heck was this woman and why did she pick Hartwig House for her home away from home most definitely was.

After taking a careful stroll around the property, Dylan discovered a large plastic tub on the far side of the detached garage. The only person who would go by that narrow space would be the lawn care people, or in this case, the homeless person. Even if he'd noticed it before, which he hadn't, he would have assumed it was junk left by a previous owner and let the landscapers chuck it all when they did the yard. Now he knew better.

"What's that?" Rachel came around to the back porch from the driveway.

"A clue as to our houseguest."

"So now she's a guest?"

He just loved the way her eyes sparkled when she was holding back laughter. Actually, that wasn't the only thing he loved about Rachel. Something told him he needed to pay more attention. People loved chocolate cake, and walks on the beach, or their mother's homemade pasta, but deep in his gut he knew his feelings for Rachel were becoming way more than a common cliché. The next big thing he needed to decide is what the heck was he going to do about it? Although, that decision would have to take a back seat to their trespassing houseguest. "She's a mystery."

"Explain." Rachel stared into the bin with interest.

"This almost looks like something I'd find in my grandmother's attic. So much so, that I might have guessed it was tossed out by a previous owner."

"Why do you think it's the person we chased the other night?"

"A child's first bible with the name Mary engraved on it signed *with love always from Grandma.*"

"Then we agree that our intruder is your mother's Mary?"

"I honestly don't know. But I really hope not. That idea is just a tad too scary for me."

Rachel's gaze peered into the bin once again. "Don't tell me there's knives or guns, or something creepy like that in there?"

"No. There are two very old and tattered rag dolls." He held one up. "An envelope with old black and white photos. An ancient *World's Best Mother* figurine."

"Oh, I remember those. My grandmother had one that my mom gave her when she was a kid."

"You get the point then. Old junk that must mean something to someone, but not the general public."

"What about clothes? Sleeping bag? Things that someone on the street would really need?"

He shook his head. "Nothing like that. I don't know. Maybe it really was left by a previous owner and I'm jumping to conclusions."

"One way to find out." Rachel straightened up beside him. "Put it back where you found it. We can install a camera like the ones you put up today at your mom's and if someone comes back for it, we'll know."

Again, he nodded, only this time, he leaned forward and kissed her lightly on the lips. "I've been waiting all day to do that."

"Me too." Her arms wound around his waist.

He was all set to forget the cameras, the intruder, the house, and anything else that came along when his phone buzzed.

"Something important?" She leaned back so he could reach his cell.

Staring down at the screen, he sighed. "My mother seems to have impeccable timing. I may have to adjust my notifications."

"A text?"

He shook his head. "The camera inside her house has detected motion. She's cooking. Apparently, this dumb thing is going to ding at me every time she waves an arm."

"That might be a bit much." Rachel somehow managed to both chuckle and wince at the same time.

"Agreed." Swiping at the settings in the camera program, Dylan quickly tapped away. "For now, until we absolutely need to watch her in the house, the camera program will only ding when there's movement outside."

Rachel hesitated a moment. "How sensitive is it?"

"Don't know yet, why?"

"Well, if it detects your mother stirring a pot of pasta, it might ding at you every time a raccoon or stray cat crosses its path. Like those camera doorbells."

This time, Dylan sighed. "So much for technology making life easier. I guess only time will tell. And speaking of stirring pasta, I'm a bit hungry. How about you?"

"Starved."

"Since I'm in work clothes, we can't do anything fancy. There's a new burger joint halfway between here and Mom's, unoriginally named The Burger Joint. How does that sound?"

"I'm so hungry at the moment I could eat cardboard at a drive-thru, but we'll have to take two cars. I'd rather not drive back and forth."

"Burgers it is then. Also, since I seem to be on a roll today, what do you say to a nice dinner out Friday night?"

"I'd say absolutely yes."

"Day's getting better and better. I'll lock up here and meet you at the Burger Joint." By the time he'd checked all the doors and windows, including the lock he'd fixed today, and pulled out of the driveway, Rachel's car was already out of sight. He'd barely managed to pull onto the street when his phone buzzed with another notification.

Fumbling with the phone, he managed to keep one hand on the steering wheel, his eyes on the road, and open the camera shot at his mom's. Expecting something ridiculous as Rachel had warned, like a stray cat, his mouth almost hit his knees when the image popped onto his screen. Instinctively hitting the gas, he managed to call Rachel.

"Miss me already?" she chuckled.

"Someone's looking through the windows at Mom's house. I think our house guest has a new target!"

"Oh no!" Rachel's heart lurched. "Is it a woman?"

"I can't see who it is, but I'm driving as fast as I can. I'll probably have to skip dinner."

"Dinner? Are you kidding? Are they breaking in?"

"It looks like the person is trying all the windows to get inside. Damn it."

"Chill. I'm closer, I'm turning now."

"No. I don't need to worry about both of you."

"Worry my ass. I'm a Baron."

"I don't think the intruder is going to care if you're the Queen of England. Stay in your car and keep the doors locked."

"Mm hm." She probably should have made that little grunt sound a bit more sincere, but she hated to start a relationship off on the wrong foot with a lie.

"I'm not kidding. It could be a meek and lost woman, or a drug-infused man or woman. I don't want you taking chances. If it turns out to be someone high on who knows what, it could take an army to pin them down."

At least the guy could read her better than his brother. "I can handle myself. And I'm here. I've got Bertha if I need her."

"Bertha?" Silence hung as she hopped out of the car. "Oh, hell. Don't tell me—"

"I gotta go, but I promise not to shoot if I don't have to." He was still talking as she disconnected the call and slipped her phone into her pocket. At least he should be pleased she hadn't arrived with her gun drawn. Still, her hand remained ready to draw if she had to. How did her day get turned so upside down?

CHAPTER SIXTEEN

This was not what Dylan had bargained for when he called Rachel. Someone as smart as he was supposed to be should have known a woman as intelligent and bold as Rachel would not sit back and wait for someone else to save the day. He just wished he hadn't told her what was happening until after it was all over.

Praying every second that everyone he cared about would be all right, the only traffic light between work and his mother's turned red long before he reached the corner. Slamming his hand on the steering wheel, he muttered several cuss words for which his mother would have washed his mouth out with soap. So desperate to get to the house, had there not been one lone car sputtering down the road, he would have simply run the light.

Stuck at the light, he glanced at the screen on his phone. No motion detected. How could both Rachel and the stranger be lurking around the house and none of the cameras track them? He'd have to add more cameras tomorrow. Damn it. This had to be the longest red light in the history of Houston.

Finally, the light changed and he gunned it. Only one more block to his mother's. Screeching to a halt in front of her house, he had the door opening as he shifted into park, and flew out of the truck. Running up the driveway as quietly as he could, he frantically scanned the area for any sign of Rachel or the intruder. He barely turned the first corner when he spotted Rachel on an old crate, peering into the window. Relief that she was safe quickly drained away at the next sight, arm raised, with a crowbar in hand, running at full speed, their intruder was headed straight for

Rachel's back.

No longer concerned with approaching quietly, her name tore from his lungs as he kicked into faster gear and shifted direction just enough to hopefully—*please, dear God*—intercept the crazy woman only feet away from clobbering Rachel. "Rachel! Duck!"

Frowning, the woman he'd already decided he was falling slowly and thoroughly in love with, turned to face him. "Thank God. She's down."

Down? What? Had everyone lost their minds? Lunging forward, Dylan was air bound when he came down hard on the intruder. Not delicate of size, the person scrambled, and he found himself rolling around on the ground, avoiding flying arms and kicking feet. Damn. What was this character on?

"Give it up!" he shouted, finally flipping them over and pinning the attacker to the ground.

"What the…" Underneath him, the woman swung the bar at his head, missing by inches as Dylan grasped the waving arm and pinned the squirming and kicking person to the ground.

"Call 911!" he shouted to Rachel.

"Dylan! Oh my God." Rachel came running toward him. "Are you all right?"

"I'm fine," he sputtered, "but call 911."

"Not you. Mary!"

"What?" He looked down at the woman staring daggers at him and trying to latch onto his wrist with her mouth. She was definitely a persistent fighter. "She was going to hit you with this crow bar."

"For the love of God," the woman practically growled. "Get off of me! I have to get to the window! It's the only way inside!"

"See?" Dylan didn't dare look away from his captive. "Call 911."

Her hands on her hips, Rachel glared at him. "Will you get up! The kitchen is on fire and we can't get in!"

In all the chaos of arriving at the house, finding Mary trying to break into the house, and realizing the problem, she just plain didn't think calling or texting Dylan was as important as calling 911. Unfortunately, she also didn't think he was going to arrive like a comic book superhero and tackle the poor woman.

"Fire?" Dylan stared down at the woman still struggling to break free, and up at Rachel. The war in his mind from lack of information was obvious to anyone.

Including Mary. "I'm not going to hurt anyone. We have to get inside."

"Do you have a key?" Rachel asked him. "Otherwise we're back to the damn window because—"

A low boom, followed by a flash of light, cut Rachel off.

Now free from Dylan's grasp, Mary sprang to her feet and ran to the back door, screaming his mother's name.

Rachel and Dylan followed as he fumbled with his keys. "Move over!" he barked at Mary, quickly shoving the key in the deadbolt and then turning the knob.

Together, arms over their mouths, they scurried across. What had clearly started as a frying pan fire was shooting up and charring the overhead cabinet.

"The cabinets are popping like kindling!" Mary called out to no one in particular.

"Mom!" Dylan spotted her on the floor and hurried to her side.

"Get her out of here!" Rachel shouted to him at the same time she spotted Mary by the sink. "No! Mary! Not water."

"Everyone out!" Dylan shouted over the continued popping of kitchen wood and growing black smoke filling the room.

"We can save the house!" Mary shouted. "She loves this house."

Pulling at Mary's arm, Rachel shook her head. "He's

right, we have to get out." Then she spotted the cookie sheets on the island. His mom must have been planning on baking too. Grabbing them both, one in each hand, she turned to the fire, now burning so hard she could feel the heat three feet away.

"Will you two stop! Out now!" Dylan had his mother in his arms like a sleeping child.

The sirens of the rescue vehicles broke through the hum inside the house.

"Now!" He moved behind Mary and nudged her forward, spinning around toward Rachel.

As close as she could get without catching on fire herself, Rachel tried to toss the sheet onto the frying pan when she felt Dylan behind her. "Now!"

Everything in her hated walking away from the kitchen without a fight to save the house, but even she knew it only took a few minutes for a kitchen fire to engulf a house and they were already way past that amount of time. Reluctantly, she nodded and keeping her hand on his back, followed him out the door.

Outside, the EMTs arrived first, running up the drive as Dylan hurried toward them.

"What happened to her?" one of the men asked.

"I don't know." Dylan turned to Mary. "Do you know?"

She shook her head. "I told this lady that Liz and I were supposed to meet at the new burger place for dinner. We've been eating together every night since we bumped into each other at, well, bumped into each other a couple of weeks ago."

Weeks? Had Mary been sneaking into the house that long?

"I got worried," Mary continued. "I mean, sometimes she's a bit forgetful. Anyhow, when she didn't answer the door, I started moving around the house, looking in the windows. Finally spotted her on the kitchen floor. I was frantically trying to find an open window, any way to gain entry, when the frying pan suddenly shot up in flames."

"That's when I showed up." Rachel faced him. "All she told me was that your mom was passed out on the floor and there was a kitchen fire. I was still messing with the windows while she went to find something in the garage to break the glass."

The EMTs were busy taking her vitals and searching for any reason for his mother passing out. Meanwhile, one fire truck, then another, pulled up, the men running about like organized ants, hurrying to the back side of the house that was now very obviously on fire.

Taking a step back while the firefighters did what they were trained to do, Dylan glanced at Mary. "I, uhm, I'm sorry if I hurt you."

Those few words brought a smile to Rachel's face. Dylan Schaefer was quite a man. She was surrounded by plenty of men in her family and knew first-hand how hard it was for most of them to acknowledge when they are wrong.

Mary shook her head. "I'm fine. And I understand how it must have looked."

At that moment, his mother began groaning.

"Oh!" Mary jumped forward. "She's coming to."

Her hand on her head, Liz Alexander blinked. "Why am I looking up at the sky?"

The EMT chuckled. "You passed out."

Closing her eyes tightly, Dylan's mom paused a moment. "Oh, yeah. I didn't pass out. I slipped on a water spill. Couldn't catch my balance."

The other EMT nodded. "That would explain the growing knot on the back of your head."

"So, she's going to be all right?" Mary asked.

Anyone watching would think that Liz was this strange woman's mother and not Dylan's.

"Can't say, but we're taking her in. The docs will want to run some tests, make sure there's no issue."

Dylan nodded. Like her, he most likely understood the risks of a head injury just by staying up to date on famous people who died from hitting their heads and not seeking medical attention.

Having secured his mom inside the vehicle, the EMT closed the door behind her. "You can meet us at the ER."

"Which one?" Rachel asked.

The EMT told her and she thanked him, then turned to face the others. "We might as well go in one car. I'll drive."

Before she could turn away, Dylan grabbed her hand. "As challenging as it is, and however harder it will become navigating Mom through growing dementia, I'm not ready to lose her. Not yet."

"I know." Rachel squeezed his hand.

"Both of you," his gaze darted from Rachel to Mary and back, "I owe you. A few more minutes and she could have died of smoke inhalation."

"Nothing to thank us for," Mary answered quickly. "Your mom is a sweet lady. I wouldn't want anything to happen to her."

"Still, thank you." It had probably struck him the same as it had Rachel, that if this woman had not been caught on camera peeking into the windows, Dylan would not have found his mother until it was way too late.

Taking a minute to study the worry on his face as he held the car door open for her, Rachel couldn't help but think of all the clichés she'd heard in her lifetime about finding the right man. The one shouting loud and clear in her head right now was about consider the way a man treats his mother to know how he'd treat his wife. Wife. For the first time in her life, that word connected with Dylan Schaefer held way more appeal than she'd ever thought possible. Two words echoed on an endless loop in her mind—if only.

CHAPTER SEVENTEEN

"Boy, when you said your family loves barbecues, you were not kidding." Dylan looked out over the sprawling lawns of the Paradise Ridge Ranch. Mingling with money, whether new or old, was nothing new for him. In his previous line of work, money was everywhere, but these people were a bit different.

"Hey there." Mitch Baron, Rachel's cousin, came up to Rachel and gave her a big hug. "I understand you've taken up firefighting now." Dead panned, the tease was brilliant.

"Ha ha." Rachel shot back. "First of all, that was over a month ago, and secondly, I did not fight the fire, I collaborated in rescuing a very nice woman."

Mitch's expression softened. "I know, and I'm delighted everything worked out well for both of you."

"Three of them actually." Leah came up behind her sister. "I hear Mary is doing very well at her new job and her new residence."

"Better than well, living with Mom." When Dylan first heard Mary's story, he was not quite sure what to make of it, but in true Baron fashion, half of Rachel's clan was on the bandwagon to fix her situation. Starting with Leah, who pro bono filed a lawsuit against the hospital who wrongly levied Mary's savings to pay her mother's hospital bills. Though both women were named Mary Benning. The mother was Mary A. and the daughter Mary E. That mistake should not have been made. The list of financial blunders that created the perfect storm to leave Mary without a couch to sleep on or a penny in her bank accounts was mind-boggling.

"So it's working out?" Lila Baron had been chatting

with her legal eagle granddaughter about another situation she wanted the attorney's help with. Dylan wished everyone with too much money to spend in a single lifetime could take a page from the Baron social responsibility book. In the short time he'd been dating Rachel, he had seen the clan not only come together to help each other out of any bind, but also to put their money where their mouth was regarding those less fortunate. And the interesting part of it is that most of the time, no one knew it was a Baron working behind the scenes.

"Best-case scenario is always when a person sees their notice of financial responsibility with letterhead from an attorney." Leah smiled. "This is one of those times when I don't mind flaunting the Baron name."

"Thank you for that." As far as Dylan was concerned, Mary had been an answer to a prayer. "I freely admit, I was worried about Mom continuing to live alone. The fire was an accident that could happen to anybody, but as her memory continues to fade, kitchen risks grow. Besides, knowing Mary's difficult situation, Mom really likes feeling helpful and needed. Frankly, that's hard for a retired senior who doesn't have a career."

Lila Baron sighed. "I can't even imagine not remembering what y'all said just a few moments ago."

"So far that's Mom's biggest challenge. Mary pointed out that Mom's hearing isn't up to snuff. She'd gotten very good at hiding it from my brother and myself, but it was harder to hide from Mary, who's with her every day. Of course we nixed her objections and now she has hearing aids. The best part is no one can see them so she actually doesn't mind wearing them. Especially since her friends no longer mumble."

That had the cluster of family and friends in on the conversation laughing.

A bell clanged like the old-fashioned triangles from western movies. Much to Dylan's surprise, it turned out not to be much like at all, it *was* a triangle clanging the call to dinner for the over fifty family and friends wandering around the back patio or playing games on the lawn.

"Ready for the best brisket you've ever had?" Rachel took hold of his hand and leaned into him as they walked.

"A little sure of yourself, aren't you?"

"Maybe if I'd been the one to smoke it, but as it turns out my cousin Porter, aside from being the best general contractor under the sun, is a king with that barbecue pit."

"General contractor? Why didn't you use him?"

She shrugged. "I love restoring, and his people are better suited to redesigning. Besides, I wouldn't have found you if I'd used his subs."

"Now that's the best reason yet." Stopping dead in his tracks, he spun around and took each of her hands in his. "I just want you to know, that day when my mother almost set the house on fire…"

She nodded.

"The fear that raged through me when I saw Mary lunging in your direction with that crow bar could have fueled a commercial aircraft. Beyond the shadow of any doubt, I knew then just how much you mattered to me."

Her gaze softened and her smile widened. "You mean a whole lot to me too."

"For the record, Rachel Baron, I do not want to lose you. Ever."

"Ditto, Dylan Schaefer."

The way Dylan's gaze bore into hers made her toes tingle and her fingers itch to pull him closer. The tip of his tongue momentarily peeked out from between his lips and her stomach did a double somersault. Pulling her even closer, he towered over her. "Rachel Baron, I love you."

Her tongue momentarily stuck to the roof of her mouth. She knew how she felt, she'd hoped how he felt, but now that he'd said it, her knees were close to giving out on her. "I guess now would be the time to let you in on a secret."

He blinked once and barely nodded.

"I love you so much I could burst."

A huge smile slid across his face and he pulled her tight against him, his lips hovering over hers. "Ditto."

His lips had barely brushed against hers when that all too familiar sound rode the wind down the lawn. "Yoo hoo. You two coming?"

A second later, Mary's voice softly carried after it. "Liz, can't you see they're busy? Come on, let's get some food."

The moment broken, both she and Dylan burst into laughter. Slinging their arms around each other's waist, they slowly meandered up the hillside to the veranda.

Approaching the rest of the family, Dylan's steps slowed. "Do you like children?"

"Doesn't everybody?"

"Not really."

"You don't?"

"Actually, until now, I'd never thought about it. But I think it would be fun to have a couple. Not as many as some of your family."

"Actually, to my grandfather's chagrin, no one in my generation has given him great-grandchildren yet."

"Then I guess I'm going to have to have a long talk with my mother."

"About my grandfather?"

Dylan chuckled. "Not exactly. But if we're going to be in on this effort one day to give him great-grandchildren, Mom's going to have to improve her timing."

Her heart almost stopped beating. In a matter of moments he'd gone from declaring he loved her to planning on children. Peeling her tongue off the roof of her mouth, she stopped walking, leaned up close to him, and planted a sweet, short kiss filled with all the love she could muster. "I'll talk to Mary."

"That's an idea." Rather than keep walking, he pulled her into the circle of his arms. "Does this mean if I were to get down on one knee and ask you to be my partner for the rest of my life, I might walk away a happy man?"

"Yoo hoo," his mother called out again. And just as before, Mary called after his mom. "Liz. Leave those two alone."

Together they burst out laughing again.

Dylan tugged at her hand. "Come on, we'd better go get in line for food before Mom chases Mary away."

Her hand tightly enveloped in his, Rachel tried really hard not to skip with joy the rest of the way. Come what may, life couldn't possibly get any sweeter than this.

EPILOGUE

"I still don't believe my baby sister is married." Arms laden with bags of streamers, Rachel's brother Cooper stood looking at the new house. "Who has the keys?"

"I do, of course." Leah dangled the keys her sister had left her in front of her brother's face.

"I don't understand why we couldn't do this at the ranch. Grams loves throwing a good surprise party."

"She does, but how are we supposed to get those two off the plane from their honeymoon and over to the ranch?"

Devlin, the oldest of the siblings, rolled his eyes at Leah. "How about a phone call? These new-fangled cell phones work way better than a tin can with string."

"Ha, ha." Leah lightly smacked her brother on the arm. "Usually when a couple elopes to avoid a big wedding, chances are they'll want to avoid a big reception. Besides, the decision to keep this old beauty for themselves happened so fast, Grams didn't have time to organize a housewarming party so this is sort of a two for the price of one event."

"So," Cooper followed Leah into the house, "what you're saying is if Mohammed won't come to the mountain, bring the mountain to Mohammed."

"Sort of. I think." Why did brothers have to be so difficult?

"Knock, knock." Eve Baron, Leah and Rachel's cousin, strolled into the house, a bottle of wine in each hand, her husband Jared following behind with a case of more wine. Behind them, each of her siblings carried a case.

"How many people did y'all invite?" Leah pointed to

the kitchen. "Leave those in the pantry."

"If you're going to decorate for a party, you should at least answer your phone." Siobhan bounced into the room. "Grams has been trying to call you. Rachel texted her from the airport. They caught an earlier flight. You have less than thirty minutes to get this shindig off the ground."

"Thirty minutes?" Leah almost tripped over her own tongue. She was a lawyer, not a wedding planner. "We need help."

"On the way." Siobhan waltzed past her. "Where are we setting up the bar?"

Wondering how she ever got put in charge of this little party, Leah waved her arm toward the patio doors. "On the back porch."

Thankfully, Siobhan was spot on. Every cousin within fifty miles of Houston showed up to hang crepe paper, set up the bar, warm hors d'oeuvres, and create a reception no one would forget anytime soon. And all of it in the nick of time.

The cake had been delivered and set prominently on the central table in the dining room only moments before Rachel and Dylan's ride pulled up to the curb.

"Places everyone, they're here!" Siobhan loved surprise parties as much as their grandmother.

From where she stood to one side of the front windows, Leah had a birds-eye view of the newlyweds. The movie playing out in front of her started with Dylan climbing out of the backseat of the car, then extending his hand, waiting for Rachel. Except rather than walk to the front door, he twirled her into his arms and planted a kiss that lasted long past when the car drove off.

Leah was all set to turn away and stare at anything when her sister stepped out of his arms, smiled up at him, stood on tippy toes, and kissed the tip of his nose before retreating again. Leah couldn't make up her mind if it was cute or nauseating. The couple made it about five feet before they began giggling over who knew what. Not hearing a single word, the joy and love in Rachel and Dylan's connection made Leah smile. The two really did belong together. Five more feet and once again, Dylan twirled her into his arms. Couldn't the man wait till they got inside to keep kissing his wife? After all, this was a family neighborhood.

"What are they doing, walking via Timbuktu?" From across the room, Cooper called out. "How long does it take to get from the curb to the front door?"

"Shh!" Siobhan glared at her cousin. "They'll hear you."

At this point, Leah was pretty sure the two wouldn't hear a bomb explode. Shaking her head at the couple once again moseying up the walkway, she had to ask herself had she ever been that smitten with anyone in her life? Striving to be the best in her college classes, and again in law school, and then working her way up to partner in a law firm, romance had taken a back seat. Now she couldn't help but ask herself if she'd missed out.

Delighted to see them finally step up onto the front stoop, Leah walked away from the window and stood beside her brothers, her phone in hand, ready to capture the surprised look on their faces. Another minute ticked by, and then another.

"Now what?" Devlin looked to Leah.

All she could do was shrug. "They're newlyweds, what do you expect?"

"For them to get inside and join the party." Devlin shot back.

"Shh." Siobhan held her finger to her lips. "Lower your voice, or you'll ruin the surprise."

"After watching the togetherness as her sister and her new husband made their way to the front door, Leah was positive they were going to be very surprised to find all their family, and then some, gathered inside.

Finally, the lock flipped and the knob turned. In true Baron enthusiasm, the folks waiting inside yelled loud enough to wake the dead. So loud, that both newlyweds took a step back before registering what was happening. For the next hour, the pair mingled with the crowds, laughed, joked, and whenever separated, would seek out their mate and smile.

"I hear you're the one behind this little soiree?" Rachel sidled up by her sister.

"Guilty." Leah smiled.

"It's sweet. Thank you."

"But you want me to get everyone out of here?"

Rachel laughed. "No. I have decades to enjoy Dylan's company, and only evening to celebrate the wedding."

"Atta girl." Leah pulled her sister into a quick hug. She was going to miss her best bud, but being replaced by Dylan as Rachel's best friend was a good thing. "For what it's worth, this house turned out gorgeous. The best work you've ever done."

Rachel grinned up at her. "We thought so."

"Your mother-in-law showed me the guest house. Anyone would think it was built with the house."

That made Rachel's smile bloom even wider. "That was the goal. For now it will be a true guest house, but when it's no longer safe for Dylan's mom to live alone, we'll move her in there."

"That's sweet of both of you."

"What can I say, I married a very sweet guy." Once again, Rachel's gaze met with Dylan across the room talking to one of their neighbors. The light in their eyes could have lit up half of Houston, maybe all of it.

A minute or two later, Dylan had meandered over to where they were talking and casually looped his arm around Rachel's waist, glanced down at her and winked, then stepped into the conversation about his mom and the apartment as if he'd been here the whole time and not just now joining the discussion. Every once in a while he'd glance in Rachel's direction as if feeling her against him wasn't enough reassurance that she was really his.

Most definitely, Leah needed to rethink her social life. More than anything, she really wanted someone to look at her the way Dylan looked at Leah. The only challenge was where to find a guy like that.

★

Enjoy an excerpt from
Just One Family

The breathtaking views of Houston's skyline were the only thing helping Leah Baron keep her sanity this afternoon. That, and the prospect of spending the weekend at the family ranch.

Her fingers rapidly tapped at the keys of her laptop, her gaze shifting from one screen to another. She'd spent a small fortune on the ergonomic leather chair specifically for days like today that didn't want to come to an end. Thank heaven she stood her ground and insisted on taking advanced typing instead of chemistry, or she'd be hunting and pecking at the keys till sunrise tomorrow in an effort to finish this blasted brief.

As much as she needed to get through this before moving on to the remaining paperwork sprawled across her desk, her phone buzzing was a welcome interruption. Maybe. Glancing at the screen, she saw a familiar contact— her baby sister, Rachel. Leah swiped to answer, multitasking effortlessly.

"You are missing all the fun!" Excitement frosted every word out of Rachel's mouth.

Leah sighed. Fun was a way of life at Paradise Ridge. Any day of the week she'd rather be there than sitting behind a massive mahogany desk that the partners insisted on when they assigned her the corner office. Then again, she did love the law, just not the paperwork that came with it. "What's going on?"

"Mitch's latest equine acquisition, his prize stud, escaped the stables. Claire told him that the family needed to have better stalls for a stallion of that stamina but it looks like everyone is going to learn their lesson the hard way. Mack is out running an errand and it only took Craig, Devlin, and Porter two hours to catch the guy. I won't tell you how long it took to get him back into the stable."

Holding back her mirth, Leah shook her head. "I assume no one was injured in this little escapade?"

"Only their egos."

The Barons were known for many things, being stubborn was on the top of the list. Of course, that was just one of the attributes that boosted success for every generation no matter their career choice. Though honestly, she thought Mitch was the most reasonable of all her siblings and cousins, so that he didn't listen to her veterinarian sister Claire was a surprise. "Anything else?"

"Actually, yes. Mom is looking for a headcount on who is going to attend the charity event at the Baron Foundation tomorrow night. Apparently, there's a seating issue and Grams wants to make sure that the top donors get stellar status."

"So, does that mean she does or does not want as many Barons as possible to schmooze the donors out of their money?"

"Your guess is as good as mine. But there's something else."

The conspiratorial whisper in her sister's voice made Leah wish she was in the same room with Rachel, not on the phone. "Is this going to make my day or have me tossing my laptop across the room?"

"If I'm right, it might make your year."

That build-up had her pulling her hands away from the keyboard and sitting back in the mostly comfortable chair, listening intently to what her sister had to say next. "I'm listening."

"You know how Gwyneth has been a little under the weather the last few weeks?"

Leah nodded before it struck her that her sister couldn't see her. "Yes. But she tested negative for Covid, and even if she was positive, that wouldn't be good news. To make my year you'd have to tell me something way more interesting like she's…oh my lord." The dots quickly connected in Leah's mind. Besides not feeling up to snuff, Gwyneth was drinking ginger ale all the time. Leah had assumed it was because she'd been fighting a bug but now… "She's pregnant!" It wasn't really a question.

"Shh. Someone might hear you."

Leah actually looked around to see who might hear, even though she knew darn well she was the only person in her office and those walls were soundproof enough to have a hard rock band practice without disturbing the other offices. Even so, Leah whispered, "I'm right, aren't I?"

Since it took a few moments for Rachel to respond, Leah knew her kid sister was either nodding or shaking her head. "Sorry. Yes. But I wasn't supposed to overhear her telling Grams and the Governor. She and Mitch want to make the announcement this weekend at supper."

"Oh, how exciting for Mitch. It doesn't surprise me at all that they would want to start a family right away. This is so cool." Leah could hardly contain her joy for her cousin. The man had been so devastated when he lost his first wife and had mentioned more than once how he regretted that they had put off having children until his career didn't take him away from home so often. Staring at the words on her computer, she wanted to chuck the dumb thing and grab all her siblings and cousins and celebrate the good news. "The Governor must be thrilled to finally get a new generation of Barons on the way."

"Too thrilled. He's already barked at Chase and Kyle for lagging behind."

Smiling, Leah shook her head. So like her grandfather to go into Marine mode. "The man does understand that having a family isn't quite the same as ordering a pizza?"

"Actually, Kyle said something very similar." Rachel chuckled. "I think rather than take the heat off of the rest of us, this is only going to fan the flames."

"Great." Sarcasm rolled off her tongue. "Guess I'll have to move having a family up a few rows on my bucket list."

Rachel barked out a laugh. "You do that. And most definitely do not miss dinner on Sunday. It's going to be a blast."

"Got it." Leah disconnected the call with her sister and stared at the screen. She was smiling so hard her face started to hurt. Rachel was absolutely right, this was the best news she'd had all year. Blowing out a sigh, she looked at a notepad on her desk. Maybe putting having a family of her own on her to-do list wasn't such a bad idea at all?

Logan Miller looked down at his watch. This day was going from long to longer, and he feared he was never going to get out of here. The low hum of the office air conditioning provided little comfort as the muted glow of his computer screen cast a tired reflection in his eyes.

Deleting spam email, one after another, one subject line caught his attention: "Important Announcement Regarding Company Relocation." Logan's stomach tightened with an unsettling tincture of curiosity and dread. Clicking open the message, he read about the company's strategic decision to move its headquarters from California to Texas. Texas? Acid churned in his gut. The rumors of a major move out of state were coming to pass. Reading on, the memo cited financial advantages to both employer and employees as well as the more business-friendly environment the move would provide.

The words blurred together as Logan absorbed the implications. A move to halfway across the country. His life was in California. He'd been born and bred in the bay area. All his friends and what little family he had left, all lived somewhere in Northern California. Not that he had a whole lot of time to see any of them, but knowing they were nearby if he needed them, or if they needed him, gave him some semblance of comfort. The idea of uprooting everything felt daunting. The email detailed the benefits for company and employees alike—lower taxes, reduced cost of living, and improved overall profitability.

Just as Logan tried to wrap his head around the news, his boss, Mr. Reynolds, appeared at his office doorway. The older man wore a forced smile that failed to reach his eyes.

"Logan, I need you in the conference room," Mr. Reynolds's tone held a mix of formality and reluctance.

Entering the conference room, Logan found himself surrounded by tense faces. The air felt heavy with anticipation as Mr. Reynolds began the presentation, emphasizing the positive aspects of the relocation.

Logan tried to focus on the charts and graphs, but his mind drifted back and forth to glimpses of the world he'd be leaving behind.

"Logan, you'll be part of the first wave heading to Houston." Mr. Reynolds's announcement snapped him back to the present. "Your flight leaves Monday morning. We need you to oversee the initial transition."

Nodding, he did his best to conceal the whirlwind of emotions beneath a stoic exterior. As the meeting continued, he couldn't shake the sense of displacement that settled over him. As his boss continued to speak, shock and dread slid aside as reality and panic settled in. Monday was only five days away. Who packed up an entire life in only five days?

"Of course," Mr. Reynolds continued, "the company will cover all relocation costs, and a hefty bonus will be included with your relocation package."

While the idea of a bonus sounded like a good thing, he wasn't sure it was good enough to justify uprooting his whole world.

"We've booked moving companies to pack everyone up, and transport your belongings to Houston. We've also assigned a relocation realtor to help find housing. Any questions?"

Only a million, but none of which would be appropriate in this setting. Instead he shook his head.

"Well, if you need any more information, you know where to find me."

Again, Logan nodded. None of this seemed real. He had enough trouble finding matching socks in the morning, how was he going to manage a change like this, moving company or not, packing a lifetime was only the tip of the iceberg when it came to upending his world. But like it or not, he had a good job with an even better future. He simply couldn't afford to say no and find himself looking for a new job.

No, he was going to have to suck it up, and make the best of it. After all, maybe Texas wouldn't be a bad place. Maybe?

Read more of Just One Family available now

MEET CHRIS

USA TODAY Bestselling Author of dozens of contemporary novels, including the award winning Aloha Series, Chris Keniston lives in suburban Dallas with her husband, two human children, and two canine children. Though she loves her puppies equally, she admits being especially attached to her German Shepherd rescue. After all, even dogs deserve a happily ever after.

More on Chris and all her books can be found at
www.chriskeniston.com

Follow Chris' Monday Blog at her website
ChrisKenistonAuthor

Follow Chris on Facebook at
ChrisKenistonAuthor

Never miss a New Release!
Sign up for News from Chris:
www.chriskeniston.com/newsletter.html

Questions? Comments?
I would love to hear from you! You can reach me at:
chris@chriskeniston.com

* 9 7 9 8 8 9 1 4 9 0 0 8 6 *